FIRST TIME IN PAPERBACK!
A DELICATE BALANCE
Roberta Gellis
"A master spinner of tales!"   —Jennifer Wilde

With more than 2... ...redit, Roberta Gellis is one of the most acclaim... ...riters ever. The author of the million-selling *Ros... ...hronicles*, Gellis has won numerous awards, including ...x *Romantic Times* Reviewers' Choice Awards. Now Leisure Books is proud to present *A Delicate Balance*, a fast-paced novel of romantic suspense and breathless intrigue.

An heiress posing as a hired companion, Linda wants a taste of what real life is like, but she gets more than she bargains for when someone tries to murder her employer on their trip to Corfu. And though she wants to trust Mrs. Bates's impetuous and hot-tempered nephew, Linda can't forget that Peter stands to gain the most if his aunt dies. Balancing duty with desire, Linda must walk a tightrope between harsh reality and dangerous illusion.

"Roberta Gellis is a superb storyteller of extraordinary talent!"   —John Jakes

ROBERTA GELLIS

A DELICATE BALANCE

LEISURE BOOKS NEW YORK CITY

A LEISURE BOOK®

March 1993

Published by

Dorchester Publishing Co., Inc.
276 Fifth Avenue
New York, NY 10001

The name "Leisure Books" and the stylized "L" with design are trademarks of Dorchester Publishing Co., Inc.

Printed in the United States of America.

To all my darling aunts

A DELICATE BALANCE

Chapter One

Linda Hepler was crying. This would have outraged anyone who knew her or knew about her because she had no reason, no reason at all to cry. It was true Linda was an orphan, but a most loving aunt and uncle had substituted for her parents. And the death of her parents before she knew or could miss them had made her the mistress of a most satisfactory fortune. In fact, Linda was both beloved and rich.

Nor did she have the excuse for crying that she was beloved because she was rich. Her aunt and uncle were a great deal richer than she. What was more, they had no children and Linda was their heir.

Linda could not even call herself an ugly duckling. Just now with her nose and eyes red and her soft brown hair mussed, she looked like a disheveled mouse. Under more normal conditions the sparkle of her big brown eyes and the upward curve of her pretty mouth made her piquantly attractive.

In fact, Linda was crying because she was young. She was crying because she had nothing to cry about. At the moment, she was bored to death. Life stretched ahead of her as a dull grey blank. The money and the love only wrapped her in a big, soft insulating cocoon that nothing could pierce. Even her wealthy and beloved friends had unhappy love affairs or troubles at home. She had not even pain or discomfort to interest her.

Auntie Evelyn and Uncle Abe were too perfect, she thought, sobbing harder. They adored her; they were warm and interested, but they did not smother her. They let her go when she wanted freedom and received her back with delight and affection when she was ready. "They even trust me," she moaned pitifully to herself—knowing that trust had held her back from the drugs and drink that were anodyne to the rich and the bored.

At last the utter ridiculousness of self-pity for such a reason checked the tears. With a little suddering gasp, Linda lifted her face from the dampened pillows of the elegant sofa and sat upright. Her face was so flushed that she almost looked as if the rose damask of the sofa had bled into her cheeks.

A Delicate Balance

"What I need," Linda muttered, "is a good kick in the behind and a face full of mud. . . ." The mutter trailed off as the word brought a remark of Aunt Evelyn's to mind.

"We never get bored," her aunt had said, laughing. "Abe and I, like your dad, started out in the dirt, a couple of worms, squirming away from the big guys' feet."

"What I need"—Linda never minded talking to herself—"is a worm's eye view of life."

I'll fly home and get a job, she thought, still sniffing but already happier. Then her brightening eyes dulled again. That wouldn't really help. She'd still be wrapped in the cocoon. Even if she could bring Aunt Evelyn and Uncle Abe to understand that she wanted to find her own position, just as if she had no connections, and live on the salary she made, Arthur Gelhorn would find her.

That was a sobering thought. Arthur was easy to resist now because she simply wasn't interested. If she accomplished her purpose and got a good mouthful of mud, Arthur might look desirable by comparison. Aside from that, if her uncle and aunt were too close by, it would be too easy to give up as soon as life got a bit unpleasant. Of course, London was no more than a phone call or a plane ride from New York, but psychologically there was a greater separation. Here in London, Linda thought, her eyes getting brighter and brighter, I wouldn't have to explain anything to anyone. All I'd have to do is write home, say I felt bored and decided to take a job.

No one would have to know anything—that she was taking pay instead of being an unpaid volunteer, as usual; that she was living on the pay. Linda's lips curved into a mischevious smile and the pink faded from her pert nose, restoring her charm. She moved to the graceful Chippendale writing desk, drew a sheet of hotel stationery from it, and began to write swiftly. Her letter was quickly finished, and she picked up the phone and asked for a porter to mail it and bring her a newspaper. Lots of things had changed in London, but the service in Claridge's had not. In ten minutes Linda was again curled up on the sofa, but this time she was bright and cheerful, perusing the want ads.

Soon a frown dimmed the bright expectancy of her expression. There were problems she had not considered. England had a surplus of employable people and Linda had a dearth of practical skills and experience. The latter would eliminate the possibility of getting work as a secretary or salesgirl— most of the ads—and the former would make the authorities reluctant to provide her with permission to work, particularly when her financial condition did not merit special exemption.

With dimming hope she scanned the wanted columns. Really there was nothing. Disappointed, she turned the page idly and there, at the bottom of the column devoted to Household Help was:

> *Wanted—Companion. A young, healthy, well-educated woman desired as traveling companion for elderly lady. No nursing or other experience necessary.*

Linda stared at the name and phone number. Certainly she met the requirements and very likely, since Mrs. Bates intended to travel, it would not matter that she did not have a working visa. Linda's even teeth caught her full lower lip and nibbled it gently. She had wanted a worm's eye view of life, but did she want to be as much of a worm as a paid companion was?

A momentary qualm of indecision dissolved into a delighted chuckle. In for a penny, in for a pound—picking and choosing would not be possible to someone who *needed* a job. If her choice was between companion and waitress, then companion she would be, and for long enough to appreciate from the heart what now induced tears of boredom in her.

Now there was a lot to do. Linda sprang up, threw on a coat, grabbed her purse, and danced with impatience while she waited for the elevator. On the sidewalk she paused as the commissionaire asked, "Cab, miss?"

"Yes," Linda replied, and then, "No, thank you. I think I'll walk."

Poor girls looking for work did not enjoy the luxury of cabs. As she set off down the street, Linda's eyes narrowed. If she had been a working girl and lost her job, how much would she have to live on? A few hundred pounds to a few thousand in the bank. Not a sum to be squandered on cabs. That habit had to be broken at once.

Her walk soon took her to Oxford Street. A middle-class emporium provided a wardrobe that would not betray her. Linda made a mental note that almost all the new things would have to be washed at least once right away because to have all new clothing would be suspicious. But I'll have time, she thought. I won't get this first job.

The next step was to find a room. One could not go job hunting and give one's address as Claridges. Linda didn't even know where to look, but common sense took her by the underground to Victoria Station, where Information directed her to a tourists' aid booth and a list of bed and breakfast places. She found a room in a small private hotel not far from Earl's Court. By then it was too late to make a call to Mrs. Bates, but Linda was not discouraged. Whether or not she got that job, everything she had done was necessary background. She had made an excellent start.

Leaving her purchases in the newly rented room, Linda prepared to close the door—at least temporarily—on her past life. The first bitter pill she had to swallow was repressing the temptation to take a cab back to Claridges because she was getting very tired. Second thoughts were beginning to gnaw at her, but she set her jaw and packed her clothing into her large cases, placing only her underthings in a used valise she had purchased in a secondhand store near Victoria Station. Then she paid her bill.

Linda started to slip the charge card into her purse as she walked toward the bell captain, then stared down at it. With a hollow, frightened feeling, she went to the writing room, wrapped the charge card in a sheet of paper, and sealed it in an envelope. After she had locked the envelope into one of her cases, she requested the bell captain to store her things and arrange to have her mail kept for her. This time, when she walked out with the worn valise in her hand, the commissionaire looked at her very peculiarly as she refused a cab. It was not his business to interfere with guests, however, and he merely watched as she walked slowly away.

The fun had gone out of the enterprise, but Linda went along grimly, switching her valise from hand to hand. Down the steps and onto the train. What a relief to sit down. Change trains. It seemed a mile along the platform, and the steps to the next line looked like Mount Everest. Ah, a blessed seat again. As she emerged into the chill dark, Linda's lips quivered. It was an awfully lonely feeling to be trudging along with her valise to a small, ugly room. She stopped for a moment to rest and looked around, her stomach tying itself into knots.

Then, if she had not been afraid that the passersby would think she was mad, Linda would have laughed aloud. Of course she felt terrible and her stomach was in knots. Here it was after eight o'clock and she hadn't had a thing to eat since nine in the morning. There was a restaurant half a street along. Linda peered into the window and giggled. Not cordon bleu, she guessed, but she could bet that her appetite would be better than for many more elegant meals she had eaten.

The next morning Linda was surprised at her feeling of anxiety when her coins went into the call box. Her heart beat faster and her voice was a little breathless as she identified herself and the reason for her call and asked to speak to Mrs. Bates. A thin, sweet voice replaced the maid's cockney.

"Yes, this is Mrs. Bates."

"My name is Linda Hepler, and I am calling in answer to your advertisement for a companion. Has the position been filled?"

"No, it has not. How old are you, Miss Hepler?"

"I am twenty-five, Mrs. Bates. I am in good health and I have a bachelor's degree in literature. I hope that I will be suitable for the position."

"You are not an Englishwoman, are you? Are you Canadian?"

For a moment, Linda thought of telling a

fib. Then she realized it was impossible. She had to offer identification. "No," she said, "I am an American, but—"

"American? Why—"

The coin Linda had inserted fell, signaling that time had almost run out. Quick to seize opportunity, Linda said, "Oh, Mrs. Bates, I am so sorry. I don't have another coin. May I call you back in—"

"Never mind, Miss Hepler."

Linda's heart sank. She thought she had outfoxed herself, giving an impression of inefficiency by neglecting to provide herself with extra coins.

However, Mrs. Bates continued, "It would be better if you came round to see me. I am at Eleven Queen Street. Come at four. Goodbye."

It was amazing, Linda thought, as she replaced the phone, how a shoddy room, having to get up and come down for an ill-served and ill-cooked breakfast, and not being able to get room service or maid service to pamper every whim altered one's point of view. In spite of being intellectually aware of security, her emotional response was anxiety. She wanted that job almost as desperately as a girl without resources. Perhaps she wanted it even more desperately, Linda decided after mulling matters over, because she wasn't used to insecurity.

Returning to her room, Linda divided her

time between looking at the "Companion Wanted" ads in the selection of newspapers she had purchased and washing her new clothes so they would not look too new. She marked a few other ads as possibilities, but did not phone. They were all companions to invalids, and Linda did not really want that kind of position. As she draped her wash-and-wear garments on strings tied here and there in her room, she found herself praying that she would suit Mrs. Bates.

Chapter Two

At precisely four o'clock, Linda was ushered into an apartment of delicate Edwardian elegance. There was nothing faded about it, however. It was apparent in the recently recovered seats of damask blue, the polished wood and sparkling glass that Mrs. Bates had money to spend and kept her pre-World War I furniture because she loved it.

"Miss Hepler, madam," the maid announced, and backed out, closing the door.

A small, slightly plump woman got spryly to her feet and came forward with a smile. "Good afternoon, Miss Hepler. Come and sit down. You are very prompt." The voice, high and almost too sweet, was unmistakable.

"Yes." Linda smiled, but she didn't fail to notice the old-fashioned lack of contractions in Mrs. Bates's speech. "To tell the truth, I have been waiting outside for over fifteen minutes. I was not quite sure how to get here and did not want to be late, so I was rather early."

Mrs. Bates laughed. "You should have come up at once. You must be chilled. Would you like some tea?"

Linda was pleasantly surprised. The saccharine quality of the voice had given her a qualm of uneasiness, but the offer and manner were truly kind. "Yes, indeed, I should like some very much. Thank you."

"Some Americans do not like tea," Mrs. Bates commented as she gestured Linda to a seat near a small table set with a variety of cakes and small sandwiches as well as cups and saucers and a china tea service of exquisite delicacy. "Will you pour, please."

"Certainly," Linda replied.

Mrs. Bates was apparently cleverer than she looked. Her round blue eyes under silky white hair drawn back into a graceful bun, which was obviously the work of a skillful hairdresser, gave her an appearance of innocence. Nevertheless the invitation to tea was a test as well as a kindness. Linda blessed the expensive finishing school she had attended before college, which still stressed such unfashionable arts as pouring tea and curtsying to royalty.

"Milk or lemon?" Linda inquired, with the teapot poised above a steadily held cup and saucer.

"Neither, thank you, but I like it very weak." A naughty smile made Mrs. Bates look like a

Kewpie doll. "I'm not supposed to have any, but I love it so."

Linda poured a small amount of tea concentrate into the cup, added hot water from the large pot. "I hope," she said, smiling ruefully, "that it will not be my responsibility to check your indulgence. I will admit right now that I should give in at once and be useless. Will you take sugar?"

"Saccharine, please—those little pills—two." Mrs. Bates watched Linda set the heavy hot water pot down gently, still holding the teacup, and pick out two saccharine tablets with the tiny tongs provided. She did not stir the tea, but placed a spoon in the saucer and handed the cup across. Mrs. Bates could not resist an approving nod, which gave away her thought that Linda was a well brought-up girl.

"No, you would not be expected to keep me in order. I am quite compos mentis. Your duties will be just what I said—to be a companion to me, help entertain my guests, make travel arrangements, write letters, and keep my social engagements straight—things like that."

"Well, I am sure I could do that efficiently, Mrs. Bates. I can type, although not really well enough to qualify me as a secretary or typist, and I am quite orderly. I like people, and I like to travel."

"That sounds very promising, Miss Hepler. Perhaps you would be willing to tell me something about yourself—about your experience and background."

Linda took a sip of the tea she had poured for herself as a delaying tactic. Up to this moment she had been speaking only the truth and she knew her manner was easy and natural. Now she had to begin on the tissue of half-truths and evasions she had worked out to support her tale of needing a job. Linda did not like to lie. She was afraid it would show in her face. She began with another completely truthful remark.

"I'm afraid I have no experience as a companion at all. Your advertisements said—"

"Yes, I remember. I said no experience was necessary. I didn't mean experience as a companion. You must have done some kind of work after your university graduation, however."

That was just what Linda had not done. Aside from charity work, she had simply lived on her very generous income, but she had known that this question would be asked and had planned an answer.

"Actually, I have done very little. I worked as a social secretary for a charitable organization— the March of Dimes—for a little while. But then an insurance policy left to me by my parents came due and I decided to spend a year or two seeing the world before I really settled down. Unfortunately—"

"Are you an orphan, my dear?"

"My parents died when I was very young. I do not even remember them."

"Poor child. But—"

The door sprang open, interrupting Mrs. Bates, to reveal a tall, gangling, extremely untidy young man. "Aunt Em," he said sharply, "I thought we had decided that I would find a companion for you."

Linda was startled, and when she looked at Mrs. Bates she was startled again because the old woman looked frightened. A moment later, however, it seemed she must have been mistaken because Mrs. Bates smiled.

"It's very good of you, dear, but when I thought it over, I decided I could suit myself best myself."

"But why, Aunt Em?" the young man asked in an exasperated tone, running a hand through his already untidy hair until it looked like a dust mop.

Linda lowered her eyes to her teacup. The question was ridiculous. Mrs. Bates had answered it before it was asked.

As if he had heard what his aunt said half a beat too late, the young man continued, "Why should you go through all the bother? You know you tire easily and all those phone calls and interviews—I'll bet you haven't had a moment's peace since that ad appeared."

"But it hasn't been a bother at all," Mrs. Bates said, smiling with determined sweetness. "I have quite enjoyed it. And after all, I'm sure it is all your fault."

"My fault?"

Mrs. Bates raised her brows. "If you did not tell Rose-Anne and Donald, I cannot imagine how they discovered I wanted a companion. They came up Wednesday and offered to find one for me."

An arrested expression froze the young man's mobile face. He shook his head. "You're a card, Aunt Em. There's no saying you aren't."

"After all," Mrs. Bates said cajolingly, "I could not show favoritism, could I? If I accepted someone you presented to me, Rose-Anne would be so hurt. And Donald would go about sneering more than ever."

"Okay. You did right. I've found just the right woman for you, too. All you have to do is say she answered your ad, and we won't have any trouble."

Linda, quietly sipping her tea, was furious. She could have wept with frustration, too. It seemed to her that she had been making headway. Mrs. Bates was just the type to be sorry for a poor orphan. And when she explained that she had stretched her insurance policy too far and was now nearly without funds—the reason she had decided on for seeking employment—she was sure Mrs. Bates would hire her without expecting references to be offered immediately. Now all her plans had been upset by this gangling, overbearing idiot.

"But I can't hire her," Mrs. Bates was saying, almost tearfully. "I have just engaged Miss Hepler."

Linda's eyes flew to Mrs. Bates, who had just turned away from her nephew, and met a decidedly pleading expression. Before she could speak, however, Mrs. Bates continued more firmly.

"I'm sorry, Peter. You will just have to explain

that the position was already filled. I don't want a middle-aged woman with corns who has spent her life as a companion, who will sigh every time I want an errand run and who 'knows what is expected of her.' I want a young girl who is full of energy, who has a fresh mind and will enjoy going places and doing things and meeting people."

She put out a hand, and Linda put hers into it at once. "I like Linda, and I think she likes me."

"Indeed, I do, Mrs. Bates," Linda replied quietly, raising her eyes challengingly to the obnoxious Peter. She was surprised to see him flush.

"Oh, damn!" he exclaimed. "I didn't know you were here for the job. I wouldn't have— But, Aunt Em—"

"Linda suits me and I am perfectly satisfied with her, so have a cup of tea and forget the whole thing, Peter. Please do."

Although it was apparent from his disgruntled expresssion that he was not at all satisfied, Peter did drop onto the sofa, stretching his long legs so clumsily that he kicked the fragile tea table. Quick as a wink, as Mrs. Bates wailed, "Oh, Peter!" Linda snatched up the teapot and water jug so they would not fall against the delicate cups and break them. Relieved of the heaviest weights, the table righted itself without shedding its delicate burden of china.

"Now you see," Mrs. Bates said triumphantly, "no middle-aged woman has reflexes like that. Thank you, Linda—and let me present to you my nephew, Peter Tattersall, who is really a dear boy, even if he never did outgrow the hobbledehoy stage."

"How do you do," Linda said demurely.

"Fine, just fine," Peter muttered. "How do *you* do?"

"What I'm told to do well—I hope," Linda retorted tartly. Peter stared, and she continued smoothly, "Will you take tea? Sugar? Cream or lemon?"

"Cat lap. Why can't I get a cup of coffee at your house, Aunt Em? Everyone in England drinks coffee now."

"Because I'm not allowed to drink it," Mrs. Bates replied, laughing softly, "and Gertrude is terrified of making it. There's no one here who can brew coffee properly." Then Mrs. Bates opened her eyes wide. "But Linda will know. She's American. All Americans drink coffee. You do, don't you?" she asked, turning to Linda.

"I certainly drink coffee." Linda laughed. "But I don't know how good I am at brewing it. One tends to drink instant when alone and living in hotel rooms."

"American, are you, Miss Hepler?" Peter put in. "I spent most of my life in America."

"I guessed that from your accent, Mr. Tattersall—and your choice of expletives."

"Then why are you looking for a job here?"

"Because I ran my capital too fine, and I need a job."

"Phone your parents. They'll send you fare home."

A Delicate Balance

"Linda doesn't have any parents," Mrs. Bates said, giving the impression that she had conducted a long interview and knew all about her new employee. "And she has been traveling on the Continent for some time."

Once again Linda was impressed by Mrs. Bates's acumen. She looked like a fluffy little old lady, but her wits were keen. "For three years," Linda supplemented, "and I can make myself understood in French, German, and Spanish, although I do not speak the languages very well."

Mrs. Bates nodded in a satisfied way, as if she had heard all this before. It now seemed possible that Linda would not be asked to provide too many particulars about her past. Although Peter Tattersall obviously did not like her or like what his aunt had done, Linda was grateful to him. It would be impossible for Mrs. Bates to back out now. Linda knew she had the job.

"I'll have a drink," Peter said abruptly. He rose to his feet as suddenly as he had dropped to the sofa. Linda reached instinctively to steady the tea table, and Mrs. Bates turned to her with a smile.

"The only thing left, then, is to settle when you can come to me, Linda."

Why, the sly old thing, Linda thought with amusement. There are a couple of other things to settle—like how much you're going to pay and whether or not *I* still want the job. The latter was unfair, Linda decided on second thought. She had tacitly accepted the position when she did not protest Mrs. Bates's statement that she was hired.

The matter of salary was different. Linda, whose monthly income might easily be greater than the annual salary Mrs. Bates would offer, found to her surprise that she cared intensely about the amount. Having promised herself she would live on what she earned, she realized that a pound or two might make the difference between laddered pantyhose and a new pair. Besides, she knew from experience that people only appreciated what they paid for. Volunteers were "only volunteers" despite the lip service of praise offered them. So, delighted as she was by Mrs. Bates's stratagem, she could not let her get away with it or the clever old thing would take more and more advantage.

"I'm free right now," Linda said, "and I could start any time that suited you. But, Mrs. Bates, we never got around to discussing salary."

It was a dangerous ploy. Linda was taking advantage of Peter Tattersall's presence to force Mrs. Bates into offering her a fair salary. She assumed that Peter's aunt wouldn't want to cheapen herself in his eyes by miserliness. She was also sure that Mrs. Bates would recognize her move and, if she was not willing to accept tit for tat, she could set so low a wage that Linda would be forced to refuse. But Linda's devious thinking process seemed to be wasted. Mrs. Bates looked genuinely surprised and uttered a little laugh.

"But I thought that was in—Oh, no, I remember I decided not to include it. I was offering seventy-five pounds per week for the first six months—but that includes your food and lodging, of course, and then—"

She was interrupted by the sound of a glass set down sharply on the tray of drinks standing on the sideboard. "Oh, Peter," she wailed again, "did you break it?"

"No, I didn't." He turned around, leaning back against the furniture so that the drinks tray scritched across the wood. Mrs. Bates cringed, but this time she said nothing. "You really do like Miss Hepler, don't you?" he said finally with raised brows. "You're making it almost impossible for her to say no."

"But Peter, you know there are disadvantages." Mrs. Bates turned to Linda. "You will have a free day, of course, but it won't be the same day every week and almost never on Sunday because I have most of my visitors on Sunday."

"That will suit me very well," Linda replied, smiling. "I have no family or friends to visit myself, so a free weekday will be best for me, too."

"I guess everything is settled then. I'd better get back to my job," Peter remarked rather glumly. "I'll drop in again soon, Aunt Em. No doubt I'll see you again then, Miss Hepler."

He left in the same rush he had arrived, banging the door. Strangely, the room felt very empty when he was gone, as if a lively little whirlwind had left a dead calm behind. Mrs.

Bates looked at the closed door for a moment, then sighed.

"He really is a dear boy," she reiterated, almost as if she wished to convince herself of it. "My brother's only child. My brother handled the American branch of the business, and Peter was raised in the United States. I do wish he was not quite so abrupt."

"I don't mean to defend my countrymen unreasonably," Linda said, laughing, "but I'm afraid that dizzying effect is born into a person rather than acquired."

Mrs. Bates sighed again and shook her head. "Perhaps you are right. Now, I don't want to rush you, my dear, but could you come on Monday? It doesn't give you much time, but I like to get out of England before the middle of October, and it would be nice if we could get to know each other before we set out on our travels. You will be able to arrange about tickets and luggage, won't you?"

"Oh, yes. Tickets and luggage are a specialty with me after traveling so much. Thank you for liking me, Mrs. Bates. If you want character references, I can get them from my professors in college and from the people I worked for at the March of Dimes, but it will take a little while."

"There isn't any hurry, Linda. I'm sure you are a good girl, but I suppose I should write and ask for references. If I don't, Peter will say I am being foolish and cannot be trusted to handle my own affairs."

A Delicate Balance

"He's mad as a hatter if he says that," Linda remarked as she rose to leave. "I have seldom seen anyone more capable of handling her own affairs."

Chapter Three

Promptly at nine o'clock Monday morning, Linda took up her duties. She was given the morning to settle herself and found, to her pleasure, that she would have her own small room and a tiny adjoining bath, which she shared with Gertrude, the maid. She was fortunate that Mrs. Bates's apartment was old enough to reflect a period in which household help was common and was not expected to mingle with the family.

Investigation showed that she could go out and enter privately through the back door—if she could get a key—and that Mrs. Bates would have to go through the butler's pantry and the kitchen to reach the back corridor into which her room opened. Of course, there was a bell to summon her. Linda looked at the bell with a most peculiar, topsy-turvey sensation.

Although she had never had a personal maid and, in recent years, even Aunt Evelyn could only get poorly trained and casual help, Linda did remember ringing for maids and butlers when she was a child. Now it was her turn to be summoned. She wondered how she would feel when the bell sounded. Degraded? Somehow she didn't think so. Why should it be different than being called by voice? Or on the telephone? Or starting work when a factory whistle sounded?

In fact, some hours later when the bell did tinkle, Linda had forgotten all about it and looked around for the cause of the sound for a moment. Then she remembered and hurried out through the kitchen and butler's panty, along the corridor, and finally into the sitting room. It was a surprisingly long way. She hoped Mrs. Bates would not be impatient.

"There you are, Linda. I hope your room is satisfactory?"

"Perfectly, thank you. What can I do for you, Mrs. Bates?"

She smiled. "It's time for lunch. Aren't you hungry?"

Linda smiled back. "I guess I am. You must tell me what I am to do, though, because I haven't the faintest idea."

Mrs. Bates nodded happily. "I am glad I found you, my dear. You are very refreshing. You are my companion and, I hope, will become my friend. You take all your meals with me, except for breakfast, which I have in bed. Just settle with Gertrude what you would like to do about that. I don't like to give Gertrude the trouble of setting up the dining room for lunch when you and I are alone. If you would bring the tray, we can have our meal at that little table in the window." The slight smile grew mischievous. "That gives me a good excuse to see who is lunching with whom along the street. It's a sop to my conscience, which tells me that it is wrong to watch my neighbors' doings."

"Only if one does it maliciously, I think. I mean, I always feel it's good to be interested in people, and if a person doesn't spread rumors or make up nasty stories, why should it be wrong to watch what goes on? Excuse me, I'll see if the tray is ready."

When Linda returned, not with a tray but with a well-laden tea cart, she found that Mrs. Bates had removed the centerpiece from the table. Linda spread the cloth and set out silver and napkins from the shelf on the cart. Then she put a plate in front of Mrs. Bates. Because the old lady was staring intently into the street, Linda asked, "May I help you to some soup?"

"Just a little, my dear. I wonder who that is Peter is talking to? And what is he doing home at this time of day? Oh, dear, he is pointing at the house. I adore Peter, but I hope he is not coming here for lunch."

Linda turned her head, but her view was blocked by the heavy drape. She placed the plate of soup in front of her employer and filled another, a good deal fuller, for herself. As she sat down and prepared to crane her neck so she could see around the curtains, Mrs. Bates sighed with relief.

"No, he isn't coming here. They both walked off in the other direction."

"Does Mr. Tattersall often drop in for lunch unexpectedly?"

"Everything he does is unexpected," Mrs. Bates replied, her sweet voice rather rueful. "After my brother died two years ago, Peter came back to England. My husband—" Mrs. Bates's voice quivered and suddenly her face grew old and slack. She cleared her throat delicately, then went on more steadily. "My husband died soon after. Peter and I were very much alone—he even more than I because he was in a strange country and I still had a few friends left. Fortunately, an apartment became vacant just two doors away, and I snatched it for him. I was ill and he was lonely, and he got into the habit of dropping in at odd moments whenever he was free."

"But couldn't Gertrude warn you or sometimes say you were lying down to rest?"

"She often doesn't know when he comes. He has keys to both doors, you see. Well, that's natural enough," Mrs. Bates said. Her voice held an odd note of defiance, as if Linda might think it was unwise to give out keys to the apartment. "He keeps an eye on this place, you know. I am so often away—the country in summer and the south in winter. I suppose I am getting old. I find that the weather affects me. And Peter at lunch—my digestion is not what it used to be."

"Yes," Linda agreed, grinning in spite of herself. "Who wants a tornado as a luncheon guest."

"A tornado?"

"I guess that may be an American phenomenon. It's a very strong wind that turns around and around and causes terrible damage, even when it stays in the same place."

"Oh, dear," Mrs. Bates chuckled guiltily. "Oh, dear, that does sound like Peter, doesn't it? Oh, I'm a wicked woman. I shouldn't laugh and I shouldn't let you say things like that. Peter is a very good boy, and he *means* to be kind."

"But that isn't a bad thing to say about a person," Linda protested. "At least, I certainly didn't mean it that way. It would be shockingly improper of me to criticize your nephew. I only meant it as a description of him—as if I were saying that he has brown hair and grey eyes. Some people have personalities that relax other people, others don't affect people at all, and still others have an enlivening effect."

Surprisingly, Mrs. Bates made no direct reply to Linda's explanation. Instead she said she would take a little ham and a little pâté. Linda did not consider reopening a subject her employer had closed, but she felt it odd that Mrs. Bates, whose sense of humor seemed quite keen, had taken her light remark so seriously. She asked whether it would be all right to make a sandwich of ham and pâté, and Mrs. Bates laughed.

"Of course. You eat just the way you like, Linda. I'm old fashioned, but not so old fashioned that I consider sandwiches repellent. Don't be nervous. Your manners are excellent and could not offend anyone."

Linda felt no impulse to laugh when Mrs. Bates approved her manners. She was rather pleased. Although she knew her manners were perfect within her peer group, behavior had changed so radically that it was nice to learn she was acceptable to an older woman.

"Thank you," she said seriously, and then, "What would you like me to do this afternoon?"

"Monday is my quiet day usually—after Sunday, you know. I would like you to go to the library and pick up a book to read to me. My eyes are good for my age, but I do get so tired reading—and I miss my stories."

"I would love to." Linda beamed. "I love to read aloud. But you will have to give me some idea of what you have read and what you like—and where the library is—unless you mean the London library. I know where that is."

"Oh, no. This is a little local private library. The woman who runs it knows my taste. Just tell her the books are for me."

Mrs. Bates put down her silverware with a kind of finality that cued Linda to remove the plates and silver to the tea cart and set out the cups for tea. As she poured, she hoped she would be as prompt and discerning in the future. On her first day she was naturally very conscious of her position, but would she forget she was working and fail to remove the plates or wait for "a servant" to do her job tomorrow or next week?

After a sip of her tea, Mrs. Bates nodded approval and smiled. "Just as I like it. You remembered very well. Now perhaps I should tell you that I have a fairly regular schedule. Old people do get set in their ways, you know. I read my mail while I have breakfast, and if there are any letters to be answered, I like to do them right after I get up."

Linda nodded. There was no need for her to say anything and, actually, her mind was on coffee. She liked tea, but enough was enough. She decided to buy some coffee and one of the one-cup drip arrangements. Then she could have a cup of coffee by using the hot water right at the table. Perhaps she would buy two drippers so that nephew Peter could have coffee too. Maybe that would pacify him a little for not getting his way.

"On Tuesday afternoons I have tea with an old friend. Oh, Linda, I forgot to ask. Can you drive?"

"Yes, Mrs. Bates. And I have an international license, but if you want me to drive you places, I'm afraid I will have to ask you to let me take a refresher course at a driving school. Americans are not accustomed to right-hand drive. I think I could manage, but I would hate to smash up your car and, even worse, you."

"Of course. I had forgotten. Right after lunch, call one of those schools and see if you can get an appointment for Tuesday and Friday. Peter can drive me to Amabel's house for a week or two more. And Friday, when I go to the hairdresser, I can take a cab."

"If your car has automatic transmission, I'm sure I won't need more than an hour or two of practice."

Mrs. Bates looked totally blank and then laughed. "I haven't the faintest idea, my dear. I'll have to ask Peter. He bought the car for me."

The afternoon was quietly busy. Linda called the driving school and made an appointment. The trip to the library was a pleasant chance for exercise in spite of a damp, chilly day and provided an opportunity to purchase the coffee dripolaters. Reading aloud in the lovely, peaceful room was an ideal tea-time activity. If Linda felt that Mrs. Bates's taste in literature was not likely to improve her mind, she admitted that she would heartily enjoy the pastiche of romantic suspense, light novels, and humorous biographies.

That night as she prepared for bed, Linda found herself wondering whether her luck—or bad luck—had followed her. Instead of giving her a worm's eye view of life, was she going to find working as a companion another pleasant, insulated cocoon? But she was smiling, not tearful, as she slipped into the bed and was aware that she was sleepily looking forward to the next day, which was a pleasant change.

In the morning, Linda had breakfast in the kitchen. The maid had not been warmly welcoming, but when Linda said she wanted to save the bother of setting and clearing the sitting room table, Gertrude grumblingly admitted that was reasonable. Linda chose the far side of the table where she would be out of Gertrude's way, set a single place, and set up her dripolater. After a moment in which the maid cast sidelong glances at the arrangement, she came over to the table.

"How does that work, miss?"

"Very simple. You put this paper in—it's called a filter—then add a measure of coffee, and pour a cup and a quarter of hot water over it."

"That's nice, miss. I could do that for Mr. Peter. He's always asking for coffee, but I can't make it. Those pots with all those holes in them seem crazy to me. This is like tea, sort of. I'll ask madam to have you buy one for me—if you wouldn't mind, miss."

"I have an extra one, Gertrude. They came as a set, so I had to buy two." That wasn't strictly true; Linda could have purchased a single, but she had decided to buy the set for a few shillings more. Somehow she didn't feel like explaining that she had also thought of making coffee for Peter Tattersall. "If it's all right with you, I'll leave them both in the kitchen and the coffee in the refrigerator, and you can put them all on the trolley at lunch and tea time if Mr. Tattersall comes."

A Delicate Balance

"That's fine with me, miss, but madam will have to say."

"Yes, of course," Linda had to fight a smile. She had already forgotten she was a lowly employee. "I'll ask her while we're doing the mail. Have you been with Mrs. Bates long?"

Although Gertrude had been stiff and suspicious even after she gave Linda permission to eat in "her" kitchen, the offer of the coffee dripper seemed to have dissolved her reserve. She replied readily enough, even turning away from the tray she was setting for Mrs. Bates.

"Yes, miss, I have. I came just before the war—no more than third underhousemaid I was then. Mr. and Mrs. Bates had a big house, but it was too hard to keep it up during the war, and after. I went into a factory during the war, but I didn't like it at all. So when it was over, I just came back. They were always fair to me, so I stayed—even when others offered me more."

"Mrs. Bates seems very nice to work for—at least, she has been very kind to me."

Gertrude nodded vigorously. "*She's* a lovely lady, always very considerate, but you'll find others who—"

She stopped suddenly, as if she were reluctant to gossip, but Linda caught an inviting glance as the maid turned back to the tray she was fixing.

"Do you mean Mr. Tattersall is . . . er . . ." Linda hesitated and paused invitingly. Perhaps it was wrong to encourage Gertrude to gossip, but she was curious and the information, which would certainly go no farther, might be invaluable to her.

"Oh, no!" Gertrude flashed a glance over her shoulder. "Mr. Peter is the kindest person alive." Then she laughed involuntarily. "Although he does make the biggest messes whenever he's around. Seems he can't come in the house but he spills something or breaks something. Fair drives madam wild, he does." The smile faded and the maid's mouth thinned. "It's not him. It's those others—Mr. Bates's niece Rose-Anne and that twin brother of hers. Get this, do that—and never a thank-you out of them."

"I've never met them." Linda kept her voice neutral.

"You will," Gertrude said threateningly. "Always sucking around Mrs. Bates, they are." Her eyes were angry. "Couple of vultures. Asking auntie how she feels every few minutes—hoping she'll say she's dying, that's what they're hoping."

"My goodness," Linda remarked.

She was not, of course, taking Gertrude's words literally because she knew that longtime servants could become very possessive and jealous. Still, there might be *some* truth in it. If this Rose-Anne and Donald—it must be the same couple Mrs. Bates had mentioned—were not well off, there might be a touch of expectation in their attentions even if they were truly fond of their aunt.

A Delicate Balance

"Yes, and they won't be so pleased to see you, neither. You be careful. They'll try to get Mrs. Bates to let you go."

"But why?"

"She likes young people, see? She never had chick nor child of her own, and she's taken to you." Gertrude looked at Linda keenly but without jealousy. "I don't have to worry. Between her and me it's different—like an old shoe, I fit her—although those two fools tried to ease me out too, saying she needed a younger woman to wait on her, that I couldn't keep up with the work now that she had been ill. She cleared that idea out of their heads fast enough."

"But—oh, Gertrude, they couldn't be such fools as that! They must know how long—"

"Not them. They never met her till Mr. Bates got so sick. That was when Mr. Peter came back from America. You see, Mr. Bates didn't like the man his youngest sister married—he was right about it too, of course, but I don't hold with casting people off. That no-good went through her money and led her an awful life. Mr. Bates was strict, and he wouldn't forgive her. But when he was so sick and he knew he didn't have long, then Mrs. Bates got to him and he finally agreed that she could write to Mrs. Sotheby, and they made it up. I was always sorry for Mrs. Sotheby. Empty-headed little thing she always was. But those two, they take after their dad—and I can't say worse."

"Thank you for letting me know," Linda said, without allowing any of her mental reservations to show. "I'll be careful of them."

"Yes, and—oh, there's her bell. She only takes about half an hour, so you'd better finish your breakfast and be ready."

Linda took that advice far more seriously than she had taken Gertrude's analysis of Mrs. Bates's family, and she was waiting in the sitting room with a pad and pen when Mrs. Bates came in.

"Ah, all ready for the mail, I see. You look very businesslike—a real social secretary. I hope I won't disappoint you. Where did you get the writing pad, my dear?"

"I took the liberty of buying it when I went to the library yesterday. I also bought two dripolaters for coffee. Gertrude would like to know whether she may put them on the tea tray when Mr. Tattersall comes so that he can have coffee."

"Of course she may. That is a splendid idea. It was very thoughtful of you to remember, Linda. You must tell me how much these things cost and I will reimburse you."

Linda opened her mouth to say it didn't matter, but thought better of it. For a girl who was in need of a job and short of money, that might be out of character. "It seems silly," she said, unable to repress her instinct entirely. "The pad was only five shillings, and after all, the dripolater was really for me. I only bought two because they came as a set."

"Even if it was for you, my dear, your keep is my responsibility, except for your clothes."

A Delicate Balance

"Very well, Mrs. Bates. It was three pounds fifty pence. I'll get the receipt."

Linda started to get up, but Mrs. Bates said, "Later will do. I want to get these notes written before I forget."

The correspondence was very simple: a thank-you note for a visit and a reply to an invitation. In the latter, Linda had the peculiar experience of mentioning herself and asking whether it would be convenient for Mrs. Bates to bring her along, as she would have to drive the car. It was a trifle embarrassing. Linda had never felt like a fifth wheel before. It also raised another problem.

When Mrs. Bates had finished dictating, Linda looked up from her long-hand notes. "I . . . about this party . . . will I have to dress? I mean formal dress? You see, I don't have . . ."

Mrs. Bates tskd at her. "I see. I hadn't thought of that. You will need a long dress." She paused and thought, then said, "I will advance you some of your salary, Linda. If you buy a long black skirt—or some other neutral color, perhaps a rose color would be pretty for you—then with a pretty blouse or two you can manage very well. It won't be a waste, my dear, because you will need some formal dress for the little parties I give, and when I go abroad, we always dress for dinner."

Linda nodded and smiled. "I would like that. I love to dress, but . . . well . . ."

"Good. Now you will find writing paper in the desk by the window. While you get those notes written, I will speak to Gertrude about

45

tomorrow's dinner. We will have a guest. General Barthemeles, a very old friend of mine. Perhaps you had better run out and buy that skirt this morning, if you can."

Chapter Four

When Linda returned that afternoon from an hour's practice at the driving school, which convinced her that she would be able to handle Mrs. Bates's car without trouble, she found Peter Tattersall waiting for her in the sitting room. It crossed her mind that Peter must have a very permissive boss. He seemed to be free any time he liked. Perhaps he worked for the concern that Mr. Bates had owned—yes, Gertrude had said he came from America when Mr. Bates fell ill. If so, Mrs. Bates's influence probably ensured his job.

"I want to talk to you," he said abruptly, annoying Linda by omitting even the briefest greeting.

"Certainly," she replied curtly, and then, getting a grip on her temper, recalled that it could do no good to irritate him. In fact, it might be much to her benefit to get on Mr. Tattersall's good side, so she added, "Would you like some coffee?"

"Yes, I would." He smiled. "Ring for Gertrude."

Linda laughed. "In my position you don't ring for the maid. I'll go to the kitchen." Linda found Gertrude making preparations for the evening meal, but the maid readily agreed to boil some water and bring the coffee apparatus.

"About my aunt," Peter burst out, almost before Linda had got through the door.

His chair slid back, rucking up the rug as he rose, and Linda's lips twitched. It was very hard not to think of him as an earnest but clumsy teenager. The tousled hair and serious grey eyes added to the effect, even though there were lines on his forehead and around his mouth that told Linda he must be several years older than she was. There could be no reply to his remark, so Linda simply sat down.

"I thought I'd better warn you about certain things."

Linda felt startled and must have looked it. "Please don't," she protested.

"Don't be an idiot!" Peter exclaimed. "Do you think I'd tell an employee of two days standing anything I shouldn't about my only living relative? Of whom, incidentally, I'm very fond."

"Sorry," Linda said, her fine skin coloring faintly. She noticed Peter blink, as if something had surprised him, and she paused. But he didn't speak and she continued, "You see, I like her, and she's been very kind to me."

Peter, who had turned away from her suddenly and begun to pace, reversed, jogged a table, and knocked the book Linda had been reading to the floor. Linda thanked God there was no fragile lamp on the table, and her lips twitched again. The first time she had come into the room, she had wondered why the lamps were all on furniture backed against the walls, particularly when there were faint marks indicating that they had originally stood in more central locations. Now she knew why. Peter, however, paid no attention to the fallen book. His face was intent.

"My aunt has a very bad heart," he said abruptly, as if he had been trying to think of a tactful way to exaplain and couldn't find one. "Frankly, the woman I wanted her to have as a companion was a trained nurse. Do you know anything about nursing?"

"Nothing at all," Linda replied slowly.

It was true enough, but Linda did know something about heart disease. One friend's mother had a very bad heart, and Linda knew Mrs. Bates did not show the typical symptoms. Her legs were not swollen; she had no trouble breathing; her lips seemed healthily pink. It was true she tired easily, but she was over 70 years old. Most elderly people tired easily.

Perhaps Peter Tattersall saw the doubt on Linda's face. "She looks all right," he admitted, "but she had a very bad heart attack right after my uncle died. She also had a couple of"—he hesitated, then continued—"little ones."

Somehow Linda felt that what he had said was not what he had originally intended to say, although the parts of the sentence fit together well enough. "I don't see—" she began.

"The point is that my aunt won't admit there's anything wrong with her except age—she admits that." He frowned. "I wish you knew *something* about hearts."

Linda had not been able to bring herself to dislike Peter Tattersall even when he seemed to oppose her hiring without a reason. Now she appreciated what he had been trying to do. She did not, however, agree with him. From what Linda had read about coronaries, which she guessed was what Mrs. Bates had had—and American papers and magazines were so full of articles on the subject one couldn't avoid them—there was very little anyone could do in the way of nursing care to prevent them. Gentle exercise, good diet, and freedom from anxiety and shocks seemed the best preventatives.

Mrs. Bates seemed careful enough about her diet without urging. A little walk now and then was the most exercise a woman of her age could be expected to take. And Linda felt that to have the eagle eye of a trained nurse on her would be more likely to increase Mrs. Bates's anxiety and scare her into another heart attack. She did not intend to say that in so many words. It seemed unkind to point out to Mr. Tattersall

A Delicate Balance

that his rememdy might be a worse danger than neglect, but she had to say something.

Linda shook her head. "Maybe it's better that I don't know anything about bad hearts, Mr. Tattersall," she said.

"What the hell do you mean by that?" the young man roared.

Linda was so startled by his reaction that she jumped and, on the other side of the door, there was a crash and a shriek.

"What was that?" Linda cried, leaping to her feet.

"Good God," Peter muttered, "I've done it again."

It was the first time that he had indicated he was aware of his propensity for causing household disasters, but Linda had no time to think about it. By then she had the door open to expose Gertrude, wringing her hands over a mangled mass of cookies, broken cups, hot water, milk, and sugar. Only the closed can of coffee and the plastic coffee drippers, rolling in tight little circles in the mess, were intact. Linda fled to the kitchen for a broom and a cloth to clear up. Before the broken glass was picked up and the milk sopped up and sponged away with cold water, Peter had to leave to bring his aunt home. Linda could not understand what she had said that could have enraged him, but she was sorry there had been no time to explain what she felt about his aunt not being watched too closely. She would have to find another opportunity to be alone with him.

51

Mrs. Bates arrived while she was still trying to press the last of the damp from the rug. As soon as Gertrude opened the door, she began to explain what had happened, and Linda had a new problem. She did not wish to tell Mrs. Bates the subject of her conversation with Peter. In her opinion, the fewer reminders a person had of a heart condition, the better it was. But she did not wish to lie either, and there had to be some reason for Peter to shout at her.

Still racking her brains for an explanation that would not cast Peter in a bad light—which would be most unfair when he only meant well—Linda heard Gertrude following her employer down the corridor, still explaining.

"I had a feeling, madam. It's just lucky I had a feeling. I started to take out the Crown Derby and then, all of a sudden, I had a feeling and put them back. Mr. Peter will never notice, I said to myself, and Miss Linda won't care. So it was only that new set that I use for the kitchen—thank God for that. I can get others from the store. They always have those. Thank God it wasn't the Crown Derby. And Miss Linda was so quick with the cloth and the cold water that I don't think the rug will be marked. Oh, madam, I'm still all of a twitter."

Linda stood up. "I'm so sorry, Mrs. Bates," she said. "Perhaps I shouldn't have asked whether Mr. Tattersall would like a cup of coffee, but I never guessed—"

A Delicate Balance

"No one can guess about Peter—except Gertrude." Mrs. Bates smiled and shook her head. "She 'has a feeling.' It was not your fault, Linda, and Gertrude tells me that no serious damage was done. How did you succeed in your driving lesson?"

"That went very well. I'm sure I can take you to the hairdresser on Friday. I cancelled the other lesson. I don't need it."

"I'm glad to hear that, my dear. Peter's driving is very much like everything else he does—rapid and erratic. I'm afraid it has tired me a little. Will you mind having dinner alone tonight? I think I will have just a light bite in bed."

"Of course not. Can I do anything for you, Mrs. Bates?"

"Not just now, Linda. Perhaps later I'll ask you to read to me."

Gertrude followed Mrs. Bates to her bedroom to help her undress and get into bed, and Linda went slowly back into the sitting room. She picked up the book Peter had knocked down and straightened the slight signs of disorder they had left, puffing pillows and moving a chair slightly. It was significant, Linda thought, that Mrs. Bates had asked no questions about why her nephew had shouted so loud that Gertrude was startled into dropping the tray. Doubtless Peter had offered some explanation—but what had he told her?

Whatever it was, Linda realized, pausing in her activities to register the thought more clearly, the explanation had done her no harm in

Mrs. Bates's eyes. Her employer had clearly not blamed her for the accident and was as pleasant as ever when she summoned Linda to read to her in the evening. She made no more than a single humorous comment about her nephew's visit. She was also very complimentary about the blouse and long skirt Linda had purchased, which she wore for her employer's approval.

"Very elegant. Very ladylike, my dear. Shopping is very different now than in my young days. Then one had to have garments made to order or purchase one's clothing in very expensive shops to find anything acceptable to a lady's taste. Now all the large emporiums sell very nice clothing so inexpensively."

Linda agreed. In fact she had herself been pleasantly surprised at the style of clothing that could be obtained off the rack in bargain departments. She had seen that the finishing and trimmings were not the quality to which she was accustomed, but she also knew no one would notice such things at a distance.

Mrs. Bates did not keep her long that evening. She was dismissed so early that she thought of going out. But where? She did know people in London, many of them, but she didn't dare see them, particularly dressed as she was, and then drop out of sight again. The whole idea of working in England was to avoid answering questions. A reaction began to set in. Linda was bored again. But, she reminded herself, a girl who needed a job would be bored too.

She had wanted to know how it felt—and she was finding out.

On Friday morning, Linda had her first intimation that Mrs. Bates's routine would be changed in the near future. While answering a letter from a friend who lived permanently in Corfu, Mrs. Bates said that she believed she would come early that year. Somehow, Mrs. Bates said, the damp seemed damper, the cold colder, as one grew older. It seemed more reasonable now than it had in the past to live permanently in Corfu. Linda's spirits began to rise immediately. She had never been in Corfu, although she had often visited Greece. And tomorrow, she reminded herself, was her day off. When she first thought of it, the idea had not been very inviting. She had wondered what she was going to do with herself for a whole empty day. Now she felt differently. She had decided to see London as an ordinary tourist— as she had never seen it. She would go to the museums and perhaps to the Tower of London. Her sophisticated friends had always scoffed at such attractions, but maybe they were wrong. The Tower of London would be a lot safer than the latest designer drug—and the "lift" might last longer.

About half an hour before lunch, Peter appeared. Linda could not help smiling at him, nor could she help being amused by Mrs. Bates's single, raised-eyebrow glance of martyrdom. Linda was glad to see him, no matter how her employer felt, and all things considered, lunch went off very well. Not a single broken dish or spilled liquid marked Peter's trail. Only once, when he crossed his long legs suddenly, did the delicate luncheon table quiver—and it was only a quiver.

Peter did spend most of the luncheon questioning Linda about her home in the United States, but there was no hostility in his attitude. He seemed a bit homesick and more intent on making pleasant conversation to amuse his aunt than on extracting information. Linda was able to say with perfect truth that she had attended a boarding school in Massachusetts, and then they had spent most of the time comparing their experiences because Peter had had the same kind of education.

He even accepted without protest the news that Linda intended to drive Mrs. Bates to the hairdresser. In fact, he grinned broadly, the expression lighting up his usually solemn face.

"I hope you prefer her driving to mine, Aunt Em," he said, then turned to Linda. "She's a terrible backseat driver, Miss Hepler—not that she sits in the back seat. Oh, no. She has to be up front so she can see all the things you don't see."

Mrs. Bates, who seemed more relaxed than usual in her nephew's presence, laughed. "Don't believe him, Linda. When I'm in a car with Peter, I'm too paralyzed with terror to say a word. And Peter, you should call her Linda. That would be all right, wouldn't it, my dear? After all, you two will see so much of each other."

"It's all right with me," Linda said.

"Okay, but you started it by calling me Mr. Tattersall. You have to call me Peter, too."

Linda opened her mouth to agree, remembered that she was only an employee, and glanced at Mrs. Bates. Peter called Gertrude by her first name, but the maid—well, she called him Mr. Peter, not Mr. Tattersall, but somehow the usage indicated no familiarity. Mrs. Bates, however, was nodding approval.

"I'll be glad to call you Peter," Linda agreed. Then she got up. "I'll clear the dishes now, if everyone is finished, and then get the car. It will take me about fifteen minutes. Shall I come up again?"

"No, don't do that," Peter said. "If you don't find a parking space, you'd better wait in the car."

Mrs. Bates's lips thinned and Linda hesitated, but the old woman nodded without argument, and her pique didn't last long. As Linda left the room, Mrs. Bates was already telling Peter with some enthusiasm that she had written to Josephine Paxton about coming out to Corfu a little earlier. "I think I'll ask Linda to see about tickets and all the other arrangements next week. Then . . ."

Her voice faded away as Linda trundled the cart into the kitchen. She put on her coat and left by the back door because that was closer to the garage in the mews behind the houses. She was a little nervous as she backed the Rover out into the narrow lane, but the car, although luxurious, was small and handled beautifully. Just as Linda turned the corner she saw someone pull out two houses away. Fortunately it was a Sidley, a good deal larger than the Rover, so that Linda was able to park without any trouble in the space it left.

She was wondering whether she should switch off the engine and go up and tell Mrs. Bates she was safely parked, when she uttered an exclamation of annoyance. Mrs. Bates had given her some errands to run during the time she was at the hairdresser's. Gertrude had heard and had asked if Linda would pick up some things for her at the same time, and Linda had forgotten to take Gertrude's list. She took the keys out of the ignition and ran back to the house. Just as she raised her hand to ring, she realized there were four keys in the case. A glance was enough to show that one probably fit the front door. There was no sense in making Gertrude run down the stairs to open the door when she had the key in her hand.

Linda tried the key and the door opened silently. Now she realized why Mrs. Bates and Gertrude did not always know when Peter was in the house. A whole army could come in, opening and closing that door each time, and no one would know. She had passed the sitting room door by then, subconsciously noting that Mrs. Bates and Peter still seemed to be talking. Was it sensible to remind them that Peter had told her not to come up and Mrs. Bates had been annoyed? No, she would just get the list, run down to the car again, and no one would be the wiser.

She was on the stair, just starting to go down again, when she heard voices on the landing. There was no sense in pretending she wasn't there, so Linda turned fully around, her lips parted to explain. Instead she uttered a gasp and spread her arms just in time to catch her employer, who lunged toward her.

"My God!" Peter cried, coming around the doorway to the landing, "Are you all right, Aunt Em?"

For a moment Mrs. Bates's eyes were wide with terror, and she seemed unable to catch her breath. Linda held her, equally silent, panting with shock. The frozen tableau was broken when Peter started down the stairs. Mrs. Bates shrank away from him, closer into Linda's arms. Then, still breathing hard, she straightened up.

"Yes," she replied faintly. "I am quite all right. How fortunate that Linda was there."

"What on earth did you trip on?" Peter asked, turning and looking closely at the stair.

"Trip?" Mrs. Bates's voice quavered and she shuddered slightly. Linda would not have noticed except that she still retained a light grip on the older woman's arm. "Oh, yes," Mrs. Bates said more steadily, "I must have tripped, mustn't I?"

But there isn't anything to trip on, Linda thought, *nothing at all.* She must have become dizzy for a moment. Yes, that was it. Mrs. Bates had become dizzy and didn't want to admit it. But . . . there had been a shadow about arm-high on the landing, a dark shadow. Could it have been . . . not a shadow? a man's dark sleeve? Nonsense! It was a shadow, of an arm possibly, but if so, just a shadow cast by the light from the sitting room.

Linda wet her lips, which felt dry. "Would you like to lie down for a few minutes, Mrs. Bates? I can call the hairdresser and say you'll be a little late, or I could even change the appointment."

"No." Mrs. Bates's voice was somewhat thinner than usual but quite firm. "I am quite all right now. I was just a little startled. Really, Linda, don't fuss. I find having my hair done very soothing and relaxing. I will be all the better for having it done just as usual."

She straightened herself and shrugged off Linda's light hold. There was no more that Linda could say.

Chapter Five

Linda did not enjoy her day off as much as she had expected, and it annoyed her very much. In fact, she found the Tower of London fascinating. In the cool autumn in the middle of the week, there were no crowds, and she was able to examine to her heart's content the window Princess Elizabeth had scratched and the pathetic words scraped into the stone by other, less astute or less fortunate, prisoners. The trouble was that a shadow kept intruding on her mind—a shadow across a stair landing.

Her imagination was running wild, Linda kept telling herself as she waited to see the Crown Jewels. Mrs. Bates had not said a word that could even be misinterpreted into an accusation. She had actually recovered from the shock with remarkable resilience and had been cheerful on the drive and very flattering about Linda's ability with the car after they returned. Nor did she seem to suffer the smallest ill effects from her experience. And if Mrs. Bates wasn't worried, Linda asked herself irritably, why was she?

No matter how she reasoned with and scolded herself, however, she remained uneasy. She decided to defer her visit to the Victoria and Albert Museum until her next day off. All she wanted to do, really, was return to Mrs. Bates's apartment and make sure nothing was wrong. It was ridiculous, and Linda knew it. Nonetheless, there was no sense in visiting places, however interesting they might be, if she couldn't concentrate. She stopped for lunch at an attractive small restaurant recommended by the guide book she had purchased that morning, but even a stomach well filled with good food could not allay her anxiety.

Maybe there's something wrong with me, Linda thought at last. *After all, everyone I know would say I was crazy to be doing what I'm doing. Maybe I* am *crazy.* That idea, however, was no more comforting than her previous thoughts, so it was with considerable relief that Linda found it was raining when she came out of the restaurant. Now she had a good excuse to return. With a lightening heart, she started toward the underground.

A few yards from the entrance, Linda stopped short. A yarn shop! She had learned to knit as a young girl—to cook and sew too, because

A Delicate Balance

Aunt Evelyn was a great believer in the feminine virtues. Of course, she had not practiced so unfashionable an accomplishment in years, but it would be entirely appropriate to the part she was playing now and would be an excellent excuse for spending a free afternoon or evening at home.

Linda stepped into the shop at once and was soon immersed in choosing what she would make—a jumper for herself would be good or a light knitted suit. Yes, that would make sense. A hand-knitted suit would be stylish and just the kind of thing to wear in Corfu. A girl who didn't have much money for clothing would be interested in finishing the suit as quickly as possible so she could wear it.

Linda found a simple pattern that she was sure she could handle and a soft, golden-brown yarn that could be worn with almost any color blouse. She felt quite enthusiastic as she started back, and all in all, her idea was a great success. Mrs. Bates was pleased and amused. If she was old-fashioned enough to believe that embroidery was a more ladylike occupation, she was also clever enough to understand that it was no longer a sensible one. She encouraged Linda to start at once, watching the process with bright-eyed interest.

After her initial struggles to recall half-forgotten techniques, Linda found that she could even knit and maintain a conversation at the same time. And when Mrs. Bates had gone to bed, she removed herself to a comfortable chair in her own room, turned on the BBC, and kept right at it. Knitting was so soothing and absorbing an occupation that Linda was very surprised to hear the announcer say it was eleven o'clock. She folded up her work with a smile. Perhaps if she had taken up knitting sooner, she would never have felt the need for a job. But it was a chicken-or-egg kind of question. After all, if she had not taken the job, the idea of knitting would never have occurred to her.

Still smiling, Linda went into the tiny bathroom to shower before bed. As soon as she approached the communicating door to lock it, she was aware of the rumble of a man's voice in Gertrude's room. Embarrassed, Linda slipped off her robe and pyjamas as quickly as possible and turned the tap on full force so that she could not hear what was being said. They were not, after all, immured in a convent, and it was none of her business whom Gertrude entertained. Anyway, she reminded herself, both her room and Gertrude's were set up as sitting rooms—the narrow beds having been covered with spreads and throw pillows to look like sofas—just so the room could be used to entertain friends. It wasn't like having a man in one's bedroom. Not, she said firmly to herself while being good and noisy so no one could overlook her presence in the bathroom, that she had any right to think about it if Gertrude decided to entertain a man in her bed, let alone her room.

Once the idea was formulated in plain words instead of being a nasty suspicion in the back of the mind, Linda realized what nonsense she had been thinking. Gertrude wasn't the type and wasn't the age for having affairs. Besides, now that she thought back on it, Linda had heard a few words clearly, and they weren't that kind of words. The partial sentences came back to her: " . . . she knows or not. Call me immediately if she . . ." That was it, as far as Linda could remember. No, not quite. There was something—not something that was said, something about how it was said. The voice had belonged to an educated man or, at least, he didn't have a common accent like Gertrude's.

Back in her own room, Linda tried to put the whole thing out of her mind. It was ridiculous, almost crazy, to associate a few words with a shadow on the landing. "I'm really letting my imagination run away with me," Linda muttered into her pillow. That's what came of being bored; one looked for trouble. One certainty was that Gertrude wouldn't do anything to hurt Mrs. Bates. She had been with her a long time, and it would be virtually impossible for the maid to find another job that would suit her as well. Probably at her age it would be difficult to find any other job at all. Still, Linda wished she had not been so honorable. If she had heard a few words more, all her doubts might have been resolved.

And if they hadn't been? What if the end of the sentence had been—"No!" Linda actually said that aloud, then muttered more softly, "I will *not* talk myself into a situation that doesn't exist. I will go to sleep. One, two, three . . ."

A young healthy body, tired with a day's sight-seeing, has its own demands. Before twenty pretty palomino ponies had jumped over a clean white fence on the sheared emerald-green lawn in her mind, Linda was breathing deeply in sleep.

It was just as well she had a good night's rest. Sunday was a very busy day, as Mrs. Bates had warned her. Although there was no mail to answer, the apartment had to be put into perfect order for the expected luncheon and tea guests. Because Gertrude was busy with culinary operations, Linda took over the light cleaning. She did not worry that Mrs. Bates might be opening a wedge to use her as a servant because Mrs. Bates was right there helping. The exquisite china and glass ornaments all had to be washed and dried, the lamp shades dusted, the lamps wiped clean. At about twelve-thirty, Mrs. Bates called a halt—not that there was anything left to do—and sent Linda away to dress and recomb her hair.

"After all, I want you to make a good impression on Donald and Rose-Anne. They will spend a few weeks with us on Corfu. It will be nice for you to have some young people for company."

Linda was in some doubt, from what Gertrude had said, about the pleasure with which the brother and sister would greet her, but she smiled and did as she was told, merely compromising by warning herself to fade into the background if she could. This laudable intention was frustrated by the arrival of General

Barthemeles, who seemed to have taken a great liking to her on the Wednesday night he had dined with Mrs. Bates.

The general, like his old friend's wife, was old-fashioned, so Mrs. Bates told him about Linda's new enterprise as soon as the how-do-you-do's were said. As luck would have it, Mrs. Barthemeles had been a great knitter. Linda had to go and fetch her work, and the general examined it knowledgeably. On her way back from returning the knitting to her room, Linda could not help hearing the general's penetrating voice right though the door.

"Delightful gel. Just what Emmeline needs."

A lighter rumble, baritone rather than parade-ground bass, alerted Linda that some other guests had arrived. The voice was familiar, although the words were unintelligible, and for a split second Linda felt unreasonably frightened. As she opened the door, the rumble resolved itself into Peter Tattersall's voice.

" . . . wasn't too pleased at first. I had thought an older woman would be better—closer in outlook and interests, you know."

"You're wrong about that," the general stated positively. He smiled toward Linda as she came in. "I was just telling Peter here that Emmeline knows what's best for her."

"Yes, but you'll never convince Peter," Mrs. Bates said with a light laugh. "He thinks I'm in my dotage."

Linda was startled. Despite the laugh and

the light tone, the remark was tinged with real bitterness.

"No such thing!" General Barthemeles stated. "No one could think anything of the sort, Emmeline, and you know it."

"She not only knows it," Peter said ruefully, "but she just loves to make a monkey out of me—and she does it, every time."

"*Do* introduce us to this paragon, Aunt Emmeline," a cool voice broke in.

Linda became aware that there were three other people at the other end of the room, now approaching. They had been out of her direct line of sight, and she had been too taken up with the shock of realizing that the voice she had heard in Gertrude's room had been Peter Tattersall's to notice them at first. Seeing Peter with his aunt had resolved the shock logically. Worried about Mrs. Bates, Peter had been checking on her with the person who knew her best—probably because he, too, felt that asking her about her own health too often would be unwise. Linda put the whole thing out of her mind with relief and turned her attention to Mrs. Bates's other relatives.

Rose-Anne was a tall, willowy girl, almost beautiful, with features of a chiseled regularity and an expression that matched her voice. The young man, Donald, was so similar in appearance that Linda would have known without being told that they were twins. Fraternal, of course, not identical despite the close resemblance. Identical twins had to be the same sex—

and there were noticeable differences when they stood close together. Donald's lips were fuller and had a petulant droop; his chin was weak, too, where Rose-Anne's was almost too firm.

That the tiny, bird-like creature between them was their mother almost seemed impossible. Rose-Anne and Donald were dressed with stylish flair. Mrs. Sotheby's hat was crooked, her hemline drooped, and her grey hair clearly hadn't seen a hairdresser's touch in many years. As she came forward to acknowledge Mrs. Bates's introduction, her hands fluttered and she twittered at her, "So pleased to meet you," in a voice that reinforced the bird-like quality.

Linda took the hand extended so uncertainly to her and shook it gently. She was aware that neither Donald nor Rose-Anne had offered to shake hands, but she was not sure whether this indicated contempt or disapproval or merely that their manners were more modern than their mother's. The sarcastic remark about "this paragon" could have pointed to an incipient enmity, but Linda could see that the rather fulsome praise she had been receiving might have drawn out the cynical description. And in the next moment, she had evidence that the twins did not intend to ignore her. When Mrs. Bates was drawn back into conversation with the general and her sister-in-law, Rose-Anne moved forward to join Linda and Peter.

"You're American, aren't you?" she asked quite pleasantly. "Why in the world did you take on companioning my aunt?"

"Money," Linda replied succinctly if not truthfully, and then as Rose-Anne sighed and nodded to indicate mournful understanding, Linda continued, "I had outrun my assets, and I like Europe. What's more, I haven't got anything to rush back to in the United States. I was wondering if I could find work over here, and Mrs. Bates's ad caught my eye, so I phoned. We liked each other at once—at least, I liked her and she hired me, so I guess she liked me—and that settled it."

"Aren't you afraid you'll find the life a bit dull? My aunt's friends . . ." Rose-Anne left that unfinished but raised a brow in the general's direction.

"He's a dear," Linda responded in a lowered voice. "I like older people. If they haven't got soured, they've got a whole different world to describe."

Rose-Anne raised a brow again, but before she could speak, Donald said, "But a pretty girl like you wants a bit of life."

The words themselves were not offensive, but the leer that went with them was. "I saw quite enough life in the three years I was traveling on my own," Linda replied, still pleasantly but with enough emphasis to make her distaste clear. "I'm grateful to have found so well-protected an environment for a while."

Donald laughed. "Wait till you get out to Corfu. You'll have enough of older people and a well-protected environment. It's a regular colony of 'em. I get to feel wrinkled myself after the first week."

"Then why go?"

Linda started, not having noticed Peter's attention to the conversation. She had known he was behind her, but he had seemed to be listening to what his aunt had to say to the general.

"It would suit *your* purposes very well if we didn't, wouldn't it?" Rose-Anne asked smoothly, but her voice had turned from cool to cold with a hard, brittle undertone.

"Oh, don't be a fool, Rosie," Peter snapped. "What difference could it make to me?"

"We could cramp your style," Donald sneered. "And if you don't care whether we go or not, how come you're always there whenever we are?"

"You know damn well why I'm there," Peter replied angrily, but low enough so that Mrs. Bates would not hear. "It's quite deliberate, and I haven't tried to hide my purpose. If I wasn't there, you'd be after Aunt Em to have all your rackety friends down, and there'd be parties all day and all night. You know she can't take that kind of thing, not with her notions of what's required of a hostess."

"She enjoys our friends," Rose-Anne put in.

"Yes, in small doses they're even good for her," Peter replied less aggressively. "A weekend is swell. Two weeks at a time is too much."

"But you can't ask people to come all the way to Corfu for a weekend," Rose-Anne protested. "Don't be daft," she added, but she was smiling now.

Linda could see where Gertrude might have picked up the idea that Rose-Anne and Donald meant their aunt no good. The maid was definitely fond of Peter. It showed in her voice and manner. But Linda was not sure Peter's overprotective attitude was right. It was not fair to judge, however, and now that she had sensed the currents, she felt she should remove herself. It was not really her place to watch the airing of family squabbles.

"If you will excuse me," Linda murmured, "I had better see about helping Gertrude set up for lunch."

Peter started to say something, but Linda had already moved away. As her hand went to the doorknob, however, Mrs. Bates called to her, "Where are you going, dear?"

"To help Gertrude, Mrs. Bates. With such a crowd, she'll be glad to have someone to fetch and carry, even if I'm not up to her standards on setting up and serving properly."

Mrs. Bates shook her head and smiled. "Gertrude has help. She always has her sister's daughter in on Sunday. The child is glad of the few shillings because she's still in school, and Gertrude is pleased because she thinks she is training a young branch in the direction she wants it to grow."

Linda could not help smiling too as she walked back to her employer. "Do you really think the branch will grow the way Gertrude wants?"

"I am afraid not." Mrs. Bates sighed. "Girls

simply do not wish to go into service any more."

"And quite right of them, too," General Barthemeles boomed. "Nasty, restricted life they used to have, poor things. They're better off in the offices and factories."

"Oh, do you really think so?" Mrs. Sotheby twittered. "Surely those jobs are so noisy and dirty and—and unprotected. And the employers . . . I read such things in the papers—shocking! They were so much safer in a real home."

"Were they?" The general laughed. "Some employers were pretty nasty in those homes too." He cocked an eye at Linda. "But I must say, I can't help bein' surprised at a bright young gel like you takin' on this kind of work."

"But Mrs. Bates is so kind to me," Linda protested, widening her eyes. "How can you think of her as a nasty employer."

"Didn't think any such thing," the general sputtered, then began to laugh as he realized that Linda was teasing him. "Naughty, saucy thing to take me up like that. I was just thinkin' that most gels like you don't even look at advertisements for companions. Ministers' daughters—dowdy, mousey things—look at 'em."

Before Linda could answer quite truthfully that she had noticed the ad purely by accident, Mrs. Bates said, "Now, Harriet, you can see why I was so happy to find Linda. She's young enough to laugh and to make me laugh, too. And she doesn't sigh lugubriously when I ask her to do an errand that means running up and down stairs."

"Of course, Emmeline, I see that, but you never said anything to me about wanting a companion. You aren't feeling ill, are you?"

"I'm afraid not, Harriet. I feel very well indeed."

Linda was barely able to restrain a smile at the amused malice of Mrs. Bates's reply. She did feel, however, that Mrs. Sotheby could have been more tactful—or was it only the seed of doubt that Gertrude had planted in her mind that made her feel Mrs. Sotheby's question was tactless? After all, a concerned sister-in-law might ask about Mrs. Bates's health.

"I'm glad to hear it," Mrs. Sotheby said, somewhat defensively, "but what made you decide you needed someone so suddenly?"

"It wasn't sudden at all. I don't always tell everyone what I'm thinking about. Actually, I had been realizing how much of Peter's time I was taking up. Between stepping in at least once a day to make sure I wasn't lonely and driving me here and there as well as doing the errands—you know Gertrude isn't getting any younger either, and I can't have her running about the way I used to—poor Peter had hardly a moment to himself."

"Well, I'm sure Rose-Anne or Donald would have been happy to stop in, drive you, or run errands if Peter found it too much for him," Mrs. Sotheby protested.

"Peter didn't find it too much." Mrs. Bates laughed. "I did! And I'm sure—considering the group with whom they associate—that I would not have found Donald's or Rose-Anne's driving any more soothing than Peter's."

"What group, Emmeline?"

Linda was startled at the viciousness of Mrs. Sotheby's voice. She had not realized that the twittering little bird could turn so fierce. There was more steel in Mrs. Sotheby than one would expect, and she could strike like a hawk in defense of her chicks.

"Now, Harriet, I was not accusing Donald or Rose-Anne of consorting with evil companions," Mrs. Bates teased. "All I meant was that people in the entertainment business do have a tendency to fast cars and hard liquor."

"What do Rose-Anne and Donald do?" Linda asked brightly, seeing Mrs. Sotheby flush and bridle with offense. Linda was getting tired of all the family friction.

"They work for BBC television," General Barthemeles put in loudly, his voice drowning Mrs. Sotheby's rejoinder. His eyes twinkled, and he shook his head slightly at Mrs. Bates, adding warningly, "Now, Emmeline—"

"How fascinating!" Linda exclaimed with spurious enthusiasm.

The truth was that she was nauseatingly familiar with the minor celebrities of stage, screen, and television, who were frequent guests and lions of the not-quite-jet-set to which she belonged. Even as she said the words, however, she felt surprised because Rose-Anne and Donald didn't seem to fit. Their affectations were different. If they had an aura at all, it was of brisk efficiency, not of theatricality. Of course, it was possible that the actors and actresses with whom she was acquainted behaved differently in their family circles than they did in the somewhat artificial surroundings of hotels and rented villas. Still . . .

"I haven't seen either of them on television, have I?" Linda asked tentatively, afraid of offending by ignorance, and added quickly, "Of course, I haven't been in England very long."

"They don't *act*," Mrs. Sotheby said with a delicate contempt that dated her as definitely as Mrs. Bates's furniture.

Linda found herself concealing a smile again. Actors had stopped being "people not to know" a long time ago. She was relieved, however, because it occurred to her that she was personally known to a number of minor luminaries in the profession, and all of them were inveterate gossips. If Rose-Anne or Donald—great Kali's eight arms, Linda thought, doesn't one ever say their names separately?—mentioned her by name, she might be in trouble. But that was much less likely if they didn't mix with the actors socially.

"What *do* they do?" Linda asked, this time with real interest.

"Rose-Anne is in programming," Mrs. Sotheby recited with pride, "and Donald is an assistant producer."

"Yes, so they are," Mrs. Bates remarked, "but

don't ask Harriet what that means because she hasn't any more idea than a parrot would."

Although Linda was quite sure Mrs. Bates was stating the exact truth, she did feel it was unkind to express it just that way. Mrs. Sotheby did not seem to take offense, however. She nodded her head and twittered agreeably, "It's quite true. I was just going to suggest that you ask the children. They make it all so clear—I just don't seem to remember."

Chapter Six

Linda had a good opportunity at dinner to find out all about the work Rose-Anne and Donald did. It was apparent that Mrs. Bates had given Gertrude special instructions about the seating, which grouped the young people at one end of the table and Mrs. Bates with General Barthemeles and Mrs. Sotheby at the other.

The basic idea was excellent and showed that Mrs. Bates's first aim was that her guests should enjoy themselves. The young people should have amused each other while the older group enjoyed their chatter or talked among themselves. Something, however, was wrong. Instead of the almost good-natured bickering in which Rose-Anne, Peter, and Donald had been indulging, there was a rather stiff silence.

A Delicate Balance

Linda knew that the group, with occassional additions, met every Sunday and knew each other well, so the silence could not be normal. In fact, Mrs. Bates was already looking toward her mute nephews and niece with a puzzled, faintly hurt expression.

"Your mother tells me you work for BBC television on the production side," Linda said hastily, wondering if she were a fool to leap into what might be a family quarrel—a place angels surely feared to tread.

"Oh, well," Donald replied, "it sounds grand, but I'm really a glorified errand boy."

Still, the sneer was suddenly gone from his face and his petulant lips assumed a more pleasant curve. Clearly, he loved his work and was genuinely interested in it. Linda drew a little sigh of relief. He was nice looking, handsomer than his sister when his face was not marred by an unpleasant expression. She smiled.

"Yes, but that doesn't tell me any more about your job. What, if you insist on that status, do you run errands about?"

Donald laughed. "About production."

"I suppose I deserved that." Linda sighed.

"No, you didn't. You were tactfully encouraging social conversation, and I was deliberately blocking your delicate gambit."

"But I wasn't!" Linda protested. "I mean, I didn't ask to be social. I really want to know. You see, I've met some television actors, but—"

"Where did you meet actors?" Peter asked sharply.

Linda looked at him blankly, cursing herself for such a stupid slip, but her quick wits showed her the escape route very quickly. "When I was working for the March of Dimes," she said, cocking her head to the side as if puzzled by why he asked the question. "A few times there were meetings about benefit performances, things like that."

"Oh?"

The drawn-out monosyllable did not indicate any real conviction on Peter's part that Linda was telling the truth. She flushed slightly and turned back to Donald.

"But I never knew anything about the—I guess you would call it the operating end of television. You know what I mean. When you see a show it all looks so natural—as if people just happened to be in the right place at the right time and had the right things to say."

A loud groan burst from Donald simultaneously with a shriek from Rose-Anne. In chorus and antiphonally they explained the agonies that preceded, surrounded, accompanied, and followed that appearance of naturalness. Linda heard about the months of scrounging for an idea, the battles with script writers, the bitterer battles between writers and actors, and the torments inflicted on producers—particularly assistant producers—by actors, writers, scene designers, cameramen, lighting experts, and programmers. Here Donald paused and cast a half-laughing look at his sister.

Certainly there was no longer any silence at the lower end of the table. As interested as she was in what she heard, Linda caught Mrs. Bates's glances of approval and felt warmed by pleasure. This, she knew, was part of what she had been hired for, and she was doing her job well. She caught another glance, too, from Peter Tattersall. That was much harder to interpret. The expression was neither antagonism nor dislike; doubt, interest, and appreciation were all intermingled, Linda thought, together with an amused understanding of what she had done.

"Wait," Rose-Anne said, "I'll show you a tentative programming schedule." She left the table before Linda could protest and was back in a few moments to thrust a sheaf of typewritten sheets, much crossed-out and corrected, into Linda's hands.

"But this is for January."

"Certainly. And it only covers the specials. Regular programs—series, that is—aren't even listed unless they must be cancelled for a special."

Linda exclaimed properly not only over the intricacies of coding and abbreviations that Rose-Anne explained to her, but that she should be carrying her work with her on a Sunday.

"There are no Sundays for BBC employees," Donald remarked tragically, and to prove it went out to get his papers to demonstrate the complexities of production. Linda noticed that Peter said little, but she was aware that he was watching the three of them closely.

Roberta Gellis

The lunch, lavish as any full-scale dinner, was extended. As Gertrude and her niece cleared the table, the animated conversation died down. Mrs. Bates smiled down the table.

"Children," she said in her high, sweet voice, "I have a delightful bit of news. The general has at last consented to come to Corfu with me. So, since Harriet always spends some time there, I thought how nice it would be if we could all travel together."

"Oh, for God's sake, Aunt Em," Peter exclaimed, "you won't fly. How are you going to get bookings on a ship to Corfu for five—let alone eight—at the height of the season?"

"By not going at the height of the season," Mrs. Bates said with a mischievious smile, "and by taking the train to Italy and a ship from there."

"But Aunt Em—"

Peter gestured impatiently and the cream pitcher careened across the table, spraying droplets over a tray of cakes and the cloth before it hit Linda's cup. Fortunately, this was still empty. By adroit juggling, Linda managed to save the cup, the creamer, and even most of the cream. With an heroic effort, she did not laugh. Instead, she reached for the teapot as if nothing at all had happened, poured a cup for herself, and, having mopped a few drops of cream from the tray, replaced everything and passed the tray along to Donald on her other side, where presumably it would be safe.

A Delicate Balance

"Damn!" Peter exploded, then said contritely, "I'm sorry."

"That's all right, dear," Mrs. Bates said. "Now, what were you going to say?"

"I was going to say I'd be damned if I spent the next two weeks trying to match the schedules of the British, French, and Italian railways, not to mention making those connect right with a Greek shipping line."

"But darling, you don't have to. Linda will do all that. Won't you, Linda?"

"Of course, I will, Mrs. Bates. I'm sure I can manage it, but if I could make a suggestion . . . ?"

"Please do."

"I'd better ask a question first. Will you be in a great hurry to arrive in Corfu? I mean, must you be there by a particular date?"

"I can't see why the general or Harriet or I should be in any hurry. Donald, Rose-Anne, and Peter have their work to consider, of course."

"Then perhaps there is no need to match schedules with split-second accuracy. Perhaps we could take the night boat train to Paris, stay a day or two, take the train to Florence, stay again, and then move on to whichever port city we need to catch the boat. Then—"

"You're as batty as a bedbug!" Peter stated with devastating deliberateness.

"Why?" Linda asked, surprised, just as Mrs. Bates said, "What in the world does that mean, Peter?"

"It means she's crazy, that's what it means. And I'll tell you why, Linda. You've never traveled with my aunts, you poor child. Aunt Em will count the luggage—all the luggage—seven times and get seven different totals. And Gertrude will count with her and disagree. Aunt Harriet will lose something different in each and every place she stops, even if it's only a momentary pause in a corridor while the vehicle steadies itself. You're going to have to get all that luggage and five people with totally divergent interests on and off four vehicles, plus taxi cabs, plus into and out of hotels, plus—it's too horrible to think about. And do you know how much luggage there will be for five people intending to stay for months when you include all the linens and the pots, pans, and kitchen supplies that Gertrude won't go without—?"

Linda burst out laughing. "Well, if you traveled with all that luggage it's no wonder at all you found it exhausting. Of course all the heavy luggage, which means most of the clothing and all the pots and pans and etcetera, will go on ahead by ship. We would only need items to be used on the trip itself."

"You see?" Mrs. Bates said smugly. "Linda has it all planned already. I always said there must be an easier way."

Peter merely shrugged his shoulders in an irritable way and lowered his eyes to his cup, which Linda had quietly and tactfully filled and placed in front of him while he was talking of traveling difficulties. But when Mrs. Bates turned to assure Mrs. Sotheby that everything would arrive at the Corfu villa intact, he glanced quickly at Linda and gave her a broad wink and a flashing smile. Enlightenment dawned. Peter Tattersall might be physically clumsy, but there was nothing slow about his mental processes. Surely he would have thought of sending the heavy luggage on ahead. That could only mean that Mrs. Bates had previously insisted on taking it with them, and Peter had baited her on purpose to ease Linda's task.

Peter took a quick sip from his cup. "Ugh! Tea!" he exclaimed. "Where's my coffee? I understood that Linda had introduced coffee to Gertrude."

"I suppose her niece forgot to set out the drippers. Or perhaps she thought it would look odd because there were only two," Mrs. Bates said.

"I'll get them, if you don't mind, Mrs. Bates." Linda looked at her employer, who nodded and smiled. "Would anyone else like coffee?" she asked. "There are two drippers."

To her surprise, Rose-Anne and Donald both shook their heads. She had assumed they would prefer coffee. It was General Barthemeles who remarked, "Usually I would prefer it, but I've had half my tea, so I'll just finish that."

"Never mind, Linda. If it's only for me, I'll get it myself," Peter offered. "Your tea will get cold if you go."

Linda was not quite certain whether her position required her to fetch the coffee, but it seemed to her that to insist would make an unnecessary fuss, so she merely thanked him and turned to answer an anxious question from Mrs. Sotheby about the trip. Then Rose-Anne asked Linda to be sure to let her know the date of sailing of the ship on which she planned to make reservations and to reserve tentatively for Donald and herself also.

"I expect we can get our hols at the same time—we usually do—and it would be nice to have a day or two of sailing. It's a good idea, Linda. I mean, good for us. We can fly to wherever the ship leaves from, which will save us some traveling time and give us more time on the island. While you're at it, chase down the flights and connections and make those reservations for us, too. Oh, Lord! Hold your breath!"

Startled, Linda did freeze for a moment. Then she smiled. Peter had returned, triumphantly carrying cup and dripper, which he set down without spilling a drop. There were so many laughing compliments on this marvelous—for Peter—feat of balance and dexterity that it wasn't until everyone had risen from the table that Linda realized that Rose-Anne had been rather free of her services without—as Gertrude had said—a by-your-leave to Mrs. Bates or a thank-you to Linda. Then she shrugged. She would check with Mrs. Bates, of course, and the Sothebys' manners might not be all they should be, but she *was* their aunt's employee, after all.

Conversation after lunch was desultory, and at three o'clock both Rose-Anne and Donald said they had to get back to their offices and would drop their mother at home. Peter also rose, admitting that he had work waiting for him. Mrs. Bates saw them to the door. Linda stood, feeling uneasy about Mrs. Bates in the crowd at the head of the stairs, but General Barthemeles put a hand on her arm.

"Peter's right, you know," he said, his booming voice lowered for once. "Very fond of Emmeline—I mean, I am—but she's a trial to travel with. I can usually manage her, though. Help you all I can."

"Oh, thank you," Linda said with heartfelt sincerity. "That is very kind. You know," she went on, smiling, "Mrs. Sotheby and Mrs. Bates will believe what *you* tell them, so I would be grateful if, once I have all the arrangements made, you will look them over. Then when someone asks 'Is this the right time, place, hotel,' and so on, you could say 'yes' firmly. It will save endless checking, arguments, and nervousness, and—"

"I would be delighted," the old man said heartily.

Linda had been about to assure him that he would not be troubled by the arrangements in any way, but when she saw his eyes light at her appeal for help, she held her tongue. A once-busy man, still healthy and vigorous, now retired, might find time to hang heavy on his hands. Perhaps he would enjoy being involved in all the complications of planning the trip. And he knew Mrs. Bates very well, much better than Linda did.

"And perhaps," Linda added a little hesitantly, as if she feared to presume, "you would be willing to advise me about what routes or hotels—if alternates are available—Mrs. Bates would prefer. I can ask her directly, of course, but—"

General Barthemeles reached into his coat and pulled out a card case. He thrust a card into Linda's hand. "You call me any time Emmeline gives you trouble," he urged. "Sometimes can't make up her mind—" He uttered a sharp crack of laughter. "Don't mean that. Mean she makes up her mind definitely, in opposite directions, three times a day sometimes. And don't let that dithering manner of Harriet's bother you at all. She's got the best sense and the sweetest disposition of any woman I ever knew, under all that flutter."

He shook hands abruptly then and marched out, leaving Linda somewhat surprised by his final remark. She had little time to wonder about it, however, because Mrs. Bates returned to the room almost as the general walked out. Automatically Linda began to straighten up the mild disorder left by the guests. She fluffed two chair pillows and then moved to the credenza to empty the ashtrays.

"Oh, look, Mrs. Bates. Someone has left a box of candy," Linda remarked. It must be a gift, she thought. It was an elaborate box, tastefully decorated with a lavish bow.

"A box of candy?" Mrs. Bates came across the room and looked at it in a puzzled way. "Peter often leaves little gifts without saying anything, but Peter wouldn't leave me candy. He knows I'm not supposed to eat it—they all do. No one brings me candy. They all think I would be foolish enough to cheat." A mischievious smile flitted across her face. "Perhaps I would, if I was really mad about sweets. I do cheat about tea— a little. I'm not nearly as decrepit as my family— ah, fears."

Linda had lifted the box and she stood with it in her hands, momentarily paralyzed by the implication in Mrs. Bates's tone that she believed her family was waiting eagerly for her death. What could one say about such an idea? Peter seemed sincerely solicitous—perhaps oversolicitous? But there had been that shadow on the stair landing. . . . And Linda really did not know Rose-Anne and Donald.

"Now, now, child, it's nothing for you to worry about," Mrs. Bates said calmly, even with a touch of amusement, as if at a private joke. "Why don't you take the candy? It can't do you any harm. Will you ask Gertrude to come and help me undress? I'll rest a while now. Later, perhaps, I'll ask you to read to me."

Relieved at not having to participate in a conversation on so delicate a subject, Linda hurried to the kitchen. It wasn't until Gertrude had left to attend to Mrs. Bates and her young niece's eyes fixed on the fancy candy box that Linda realized she was still carrying it. Her immediate reaction was to offer the whole thing to the girl, but then she felt Mrs. Bates might be offended by that. She put the box on the table.

"Would you like some?" Linda asked. "Mrs.

Bates says she isn't allowed to eat it and we can have it."

"Oh, thank you, miss. I would like a piece, but I'll just finish this washing up first so I can dry my hands."

Linda smiled. "What's your name? Everyone keeps saying Gertrude's niece, and I can't very well call you that."

"You might as well," the girl replied, giggling in a far more casual way than her aunt would ever use. "My name's Gertrude, too. But you can call me Gert. Most people do."

Automatically, Linda picked up a towel and began to dry cups.

"You'd better not," Gert said after a surprised glance. "Auntie will kill me. It's not your place to dry dishes in Auntie's kitchen."

Linda glanced at her watch. "It takes about half an hour. I'll dry till I hear your aunt coming. It's odd how things change. You don't really think it's out of place for me to help dry dishes, and neither do I."

" 'Course not. These days it's different. Only the older people have those notions. You know, I don't think my aunt could be in service in a modern household. Not that it matters. She won't work any more after Mrs. Bates dies. She's going to get something handsome in the old lady's will, and she has plenty of her own saved, too."

"I guess she's attached to Mrs. Bates."

"Very. Well, that's done. Now I'll put away what you've dried and we'll be finished."

A little while later, when Gertrude came back

down the corridor, Gert was munching her fourth piece of candy and Linda was checking the coffee supply.

"Can I help you, Miss?" Gertrude asked.

"I was just checking to make sure that there will be enough coffee for tomorrow," Linda said. "Do you think we should buy a large can next time?"

Gertrude pursed her lips in thought, and for a few minutes they discussed the probable rate of use of coffee, including General Barthemeles as a drinker now that he knew the beverage was available. Then Gertrude asked whether there were larger versions of the dripolater.

"I nearly had a heart attack when Mr. Peter carried that contraption full of grounds and hot water into the dining room. I was sure I'd be cleaning the carpet again. But if I could make a pot, it could go out on the tray with the tea."

Linda laughed and agreed to look for a four-cup cone and set of filters, aware that while she was talking, Gertrude's eyes had flashed here and there about the kitchen checking on what had been done and left undone. Finally, satisfied with the state of the sink and counters, Gertrude looked at her niece, who was sitting at the table in a somewhat slumped position, reaching toward the candy box again.

"What are you doing, Gert?" Gertrude asked sharply.

"Miss Linda offered me some candy," the girl said slowly, seeming to lift her head with an effort. "She said Mrs. Bates had given her the box . . . Oh, I *do* feel funny."

"What do you mean—funny?" Gertrude asked, moving closer.

Gert blinked her eyes exaggeratedly, as if the lids were too heavy to move easily, shook her head, and half rose, her lips parted as if she intended to reply but could not. She never made it to her feet, but toppled slowly sideways. Had not Gertrude caught her, she would have fallen heavily. Linda leapt to help, and together they supported the girl into Gertrude's room and laid her on the bed.

Gertrude shut the door before asking, "What happened?"

"I don't know," Linda replied, eyes wide with shock. "Mrs. Bates told me to fetch you, and I did. I asked Gert's name and offered her some candy. When she finished washing up, she sat down at the table and ate a couple of pieces of the candy while we talked. Up till then she was fine. She didn't say a word about feeling sick. Oh, Gertrude, let's call her doctor. Does she faint often?"

"She never fainted in her life that I know of." Gertrude herself was white. "She was bright enough when she came in—and she would have told me quick enough if she didn't feel good. She's a good girl, but not one to do more than she has to. I don't even know who her doctor is—and he wouldn't come here, anyway. It's right out of his territory."

"Then let's call Mrs. Bates's doctor. We must call someone."

"Mrs. Bates's doctor! Oh, no! That's not right, and besides, look at her. Her breathing is good and her color is good. She looks as if she's asleep—just as if she fell asleep."

"But Gertrude, people don't fall asleep in the middle of a conversation like that."

Linda was trembling with fear. She had seen people who looked asleep, who had good color and quiet breathing at first, but who drifted deeper and deeper until they were in irreversible coma. Her friends had not been immune from the drug epidemic and its tragedies. But Gert was no drug-taker. Linda was almost prepared to swear to that, and she had taken nothing, eaten and drunk nothing—except the candy. The candy!

Meanwhile Gertrude had been shaking her niece roughly. Gert's eyes opened and rolled around vaguely. "What's the matter with you?" Gertrude shouted. "Sit up! Come on, sit up!"

With help, Gert managed this. Her eyes kept closing, and she mumbled protests, but Gertrude forced her to her feet and, with Linda helping, started her niece in a staggering walk around and around the small room.

"Gertrude," Linda whispered in a frightened voice, "it's the candy. Someone left that candy for Mrs. Bates. It has to be the candy. We must call a doctor. We must tell Mrs. Bates."

Over Gert's wobbling head, Gertrude stared at Linda. "Oh, no, miss. Oh, no. No one would . . . Oh, no, no!" Desperately, Gertrude slapped her niece's face. "Gert! You feel better, don't you? Don't you?"

"Feel okay," Gert muttered. "Sleepy. Want to sleep. Auntie, lemme sleep."

The reply seemed to steady Gertrude. "Maybe we do have to tell madam, but not now when she's tired." Her eyes filled with tears. "I know something about this. My brother's boy, he took something once. We got to keep her walking. She be all right as long as she can walk."

"But Gertrude—" Linda sobbed, bit her lips, and swallowed. "If it was the candy—"

"No one will get nothing into this house again," Gertrude snarled. "Don't you worry about that! Listen, Miss Linda, this kind of trouble will kill madam. You know what we'll have if you call a doctor? The police, asking questions. The newspapers sniffing around all the time, yelling attempted murder. I think madam would *rather* be dead than have that kind of noise about her family."

"You don't seem to understand," Linda snapped, outrage replacing her fear. "If it was the candy, do you think it will stop there? Anyone who would do such a thing is crazy. That person will try again. And Mrs. Bates *will* be dead."

"Not if you and I watch close," Gertrude said stubbornly. "Besides, what if it isn't the candy? Maybe Gert took something before you came in. I won't have another case in my family. I can afford to have her taken care of quiet."

Linda drew a trembling breath. Gert was still walking and perhaps was even a little steadier on her feet. "I'll make some strong coffee," she said. "That will help. Can you manage her alone?"

"I think so. I'll call if I need you. Thank you, Miss Linda."

"I hope we won't both have cause to curse me soon for giving in," Linda muttered as she walked into the kitchen.

Her eyes, drawn immediately to the table, flinched away, flashed back, and then bulged. There was nothing on the table! The box of candy was gone!

"Gertrude!" Linda rushed back to the maid's room, barely restraining herself from screaming. "The candy is gone!"

"Gone?" Gertrude thrust Gert into Linda's arms and took off, almost running.

In the ten or fifteen minutes the maid was away, Linda felt as if she had aged years. The only reason she did not ignore everything Gertrude had said and call the police was that Gert seemed to be improving steadily. Although her head still lolled sometimes, often she held it upright and she didn't seem to lean as heavily on Linda or stagger so much.

Gertrude returned, her face hard, her lips compressed into a tight line. "It's all right, Miss Linda," she said stiffly. "It's best you forget the whole thing. Don't mention it to madam. She knows . . ." For a moment her face crumpled, as if she were about to cry, but she did not. "Madam took the box." Her voice shook, but she cleared her throat and went on more steadily,

"She smashed up all the candies and flushed them down her loo." Gertrude pressed a hand to her face. "There's nothing either of us can do now, so it's best to forget it."

Chapter Seven

Although Gert suffered no ill effects—a couple of cups of strong coffee and some more walking returned her to normal—and she seemed content with the explanation of "bad" candy that Gertrude offered, Linda was badly upset. She hardly slept at all that night, her thoughts squirrelling round and round, conscience battling with doubt.

Who had left that candy? Anyone could have slipped it out of a briefcase or from under a newspaper on the credenza. Was there something in the candy? Or had Gert taken some drug before she came with which the sugar had reacted? No, that was nonsense. Mrs. Bates would not have gotten rid of the candy if it was innocent. But how had Mrs. Bates known it was drugged? At least it was only a drug, not

poison—Gert had suffered no pain or nausea—
and whatever it was, the amount must have been
small. Gert had eaten four pieces, and the effect
had worn off pretty quickly. But Gert was young
and healthy. What effect would even that small
amount have had on Mrs. Bates, who had a
weak heart? Or did Mrs. Bates have a weak
heart? Peter said so, but Mrs. Bates didn't look
or act as if her heart was weak.

Why were Gertrude and Mrs. Bates so dead
set against finding out about that candy? Family
loyalty was a great thing, but it could be carried
too far. Or, if Mrs. Bates had been suspicious
of the "gift," why did she give it to me? Linda
wondered. And why destroy it in such a surreptitious manner?

But none of the questions was quite as important to Linda as the one regarding her own
behavior. She could understand why she had
not called a doctor when Gert first reacted.
She knew she had been so shocked that she
was not thinking clearly. But now, considering
the matter in relative calm, it was necessary to
decide what action to take.

Linda's first instinct had been to go to the
police. Even though she had no evidence
because she was sure Gertrude had given
Gert the torn-up candy box to dispose of
elsewhere, even though Gertrude and Mrs.
Bates would both probably deny what she
said and Mrs. Bates would almost certainly
dismiss her, the police would have a record of
the complaint. Then, if Mrs. Bates should die

soon, Linda thought, they would investigate.

Eventually she was forced to give up that idea. Mrs. Bates was old. Perhaps she did have a bad heart. The likelihood of the police ever hearing of her death was very small. In all probability her own doctor would issue the death certificate. Whoever left that candy was clever. Linda was sure there would be no obvious sign of foul play, and the police were not notified of cases of natural death.

Then Linda thought of telling Peter. The moment the idea came to her, she felt better. Her lips began to curve into a smile. The thought of Peter was accompanied by the tinkle of shattered glass and the creak of rocking furniture. Nonetheless it was a bright, stimulating idea, warm, comfortable, and utterly delightful.

The first shadow on the brightness was purely practical. It would be hard to speak to Peter alone in Mrs. Bates's apartment for long enough to explain the complicated story. Linda knew he lived on the same street, but not which house. Nor did she know the name of his place of business. She could not ask Gertrude, and she could not endure waiting until he dropped in and she could ask. She had to tell someone right away.

The phone book. Peter must have a telephone. His address—Oh, Lord, what was she thinking of? What if *Peter* had left the candy? Every instinct Linda had recoiled from that notion. If he had done it, it was a deliberate attempt at murder. He knew of his aunt's weak heart. He knew she must not eat sweets. It wasn't, couldn't be, true—yet there had been the shadow of an arm across the stairwell . . . or had there been?

The best thing to do—Linda formulated her thoughts into words deliberately—was to tell him and see how he acted and what he said. That would clear up everything.

"Oh, no, it won't," Linda whispered into the dark.

If Peter had left the candy—whoever had left the candy—he would be prepared for anything. Anyone would look shocked and alarmed. And who could tell whether the emotions were real? Linda did not have that much faith in her ability to judge character or reactions. He could urge her to tell the police. He would be under no greater suspicion than anyone else, and Linda would be fired—which might be what he wanted. And if he urged her not to tell, it might not mean he was guilty. Like Gertrude, he might wish to spare his aunt the grief and trouble of an investigation. Gertrude said—

That name caught Linda's mind. So much depended on what Gertrude said. Gertrude said Mrs. Bates did not want Linda to discuss the matter with her. Gertrude said Mrs. Bates had already destroyed the candy. Gertrude said Mrs. Bates knew the candy was harmful. Gertrude said! And Gertrude had been furious when she saw Gert reaching for a piece of the candy. Why? Did she know what was in it? Gertrude was due for "something handsome" in Mrs. Bates's will. Had she—

"Stop it!" Linda hissed at herself. "Stop it! Next you'll be thinking of reasons why you would have left the candy."

Gertrude was devoted to Mrs. Bates. She had been with her for years. She was well paid and treated with consideration—at least, that was what Gertrude said. Could Gertrude and Peter be in league? What was that late-night conference about?

How can I know? Linda wondered, twisting restlessly in bed. She didn't really know any of these people. If she knew them better, if she could talk to someone who knew them and who *couldn't* gain anything by Mrs. Bates's death— Linda's mind checked over the people at the dinner party, but they were all related. No, the general wasn't related. He wasn't even originally Mrs. Bates's friend. Linda remembered Mrs. Bates telling her that General Barthemeles had been her husband's friend. Surely he would have nothing to gain by Mrs. Bates's death. Linda thought about his clothing and the finely engraved card he had given her. He had means of his own. The general. Linda sighed with relief. Her eyes closed. At last she slept.

If Linda had ever been in any doubt about Mrs. Bates's shrewdness, the events of Monday would have wiped it out. She had scarcely had time to finish her breakfast coffee when she was summoned to Mrs. Bates's bedroom. The old lady looked even more like a Kewpie doll in her frilled bedjacket, and she sighed when Linda came in.

"You look tired, my dear. I suppose you lay awake half the night worrying about what happened. Now that was very foolish. I told you I am able to take care of myself. Now don't turn into another Peter, forever telling me what to do and worrying about me."

"But—"

"No buts. You don't know what happened, but I do. I'm sorry I was a little slow in realizing it so that you got a fright, but I assure you it was only a piece of naughty mischief. I won't tell you who perpetrated it or why because"—she paused, looked at Linda, and shook her head—"you are no actress, and your attitude toward the person would change. That would show, and I wouldn't want that, especially since I know that no harm was intended. In fact, the intention was good, even though the method was terribly foolish."

"The intention was good?" Linda echoed unbelievingly.

Mrs. Bates laughed. "Yes. Now do stop thinking about it. I assure you nothing like that will ever happen again. I'll have a word with that silly—Never you mind. Now the first thing you must do is write to Josephine Paxton for me. She is to tell the caretakers to get the villa ready and also let the housekeeper know that the heavy luggage will be shipped ahead this time." A shadow crossed her face and she said with a small quaver, "Shipping separately will be safe, won't it?"

"Indeed it will—unless the ship sinks—and you wouldn't want to be aboard then," Linda said, smiling. "Everything will be crated and insured." She stopped abruptly, barely swallowing the information that her Aunt Evelyn regularly shipped articles to her house in the south of Spain.

"Yes, of course." Mrs. Bates did not seem to have noticed the awkward stop. "You will then have to let Josephine know by telephone or cable the exact date that we will arrive and the name of the ship on which the baggage will come as soon as you have completed the arrangements. She will have to arrange to check that everything has arrived safely—of course you will have to make a list and send that—and see that my things are transported to the villa. Put in the proper number of pleases and thank-yous for me."

"Yes, Mrs. Bates."

"As soon as you have finished writing, you had better go to the steamship and train offices. You may take the car if you think that will be more convenient, or I will reimburse you for underground and cab fares."

"Rose-Anne asked whether I would make plane reservations for her and Donald while I was doing the rest of the travel work."

Mrs. Bates tskd, but good-humoredly. "Lazy children! I suppose she told you to do it as if you were a messenger girl, too. I don't know how Harriet raised those children, but she certainly didn't teach them manners. Well—if you don't mind, Linda, it would simplify matters. But if you prefer not to bother, just tell Rose-Anne to do her own dirty work."

Linda smiled. She had felt a trifle resentful, but Mrs. Bates's understanding had removed the sting completely. "I don't mind at all. I was a little annoyed, I'll admit," she confessed, "but thinking back on it, I don't believe Rose-Anne meant to be rude. She's an efficient person, and I suppose she has a secretary. She asked me because it was reasonable for me to make the reservations at the same time; the way she asked was the way she gives orders to the secretary."

"You are a sweet child. I won't wait lunch for you, so eat out if you are out at lunch time. I'll pay for that, of course. Now, if you aren't too tired when you get back, telephone a place called Handy Andy—silly name, isn't it? They provide men who do odd jobs. Get someone to take the trunks out of the cellar and clean them thoroughly so that Gertrude can start packing whenever she has the time."

"Yes, Mrs. Bates."

"And you will have to number the trunks or label them in some way so you can list the contents. I am sorry to say it, but the people on Corfu are very skilled at opening simple trunk locks and extracting any contents that are valuable or that may strike their fancy."

"They'll have a much harder time because the trunks will be in crates, but if you are concerned, I'll insure the contents individually."

"That will mean a duplicate list, I'm afraid."

"I'll do the lists in quintuplicate, Mrs. Bates. It isn't any more trouble to print five copies than to print two, and that way I can send Mrs. Paxton a list, have two for us, and one each for the insurance company and the shipping line."

"Now that's very clever, Linda. It never hurts to have an extra copy or two. Do you have your own typewriter?"

"Oh, no, I don't," Linda said, recalling with longing the little laptop computer and portable printer locked in her luggage. "I thought—"

Mrs. Bates laughed. "Now what would I do with a typewriter? However, that can't be any trouble. Anything can be rented these days. I'm sure you could rent a typewriter, or whatever you need, for a week or two. But you will have to see about that. My, you do have a heavy schedule. But do you think you could find time to get to the library and pick up some new books for me?"

"Of course I can."

"Then that's all I can think of just now, Linda." Mrs. Bates's eyes twinkled. "But I am sure I will have a whole new list by the time you get home."

Linda smiled too. It was perfectly obvious that Mrs. Bates intended to keep her too busy to worry until she was over the shock of the candy incident. It was done so openly, however, that Linda could not believe Mrs. Bates was trying to deceive her. Clearly her employer was neither worried nor frightened. She was merely trying to restore Linda's peace of mind. And, Linda thought as she left Mrs. Bates's room, perhaps she was right. *Perhaps I'm making a mountain out of a molehill. After all, I really don't know these people.*

However, neither that idea nor the fact that she was forced to stop thinking about the problem while she wrote to Mrs. Paxton made the "prank" any easier to accept. Linda acknowledged that whoever left the candy knew Mrs. Bates well enough to be sure she wouldn't eat it and therefore would be in no danger—but then, what could be the purpose of the "gift"? Linda had just put out her hand to take her coat from the closet when the answer came to her and she froze.

She was the target! She, Linda, had been the target of the drugged candy because whoever left it knew Mrs. Bates would offer it to her. But that was insane! No one knew her well enough to want to hurt her. Linda drew breath slowly, her soft brown eyes taking on the hard glitter of agates between her narrowed lids. Not to hurt her. Of course there had been no intention of harming her in any way. She could have eaten the whole box of candy without being in any serious physical danger. Someone wanted to frighten her. She was in someone's way and the threat was meant to drive her away.

Linda's pretty face turned quite hard, and her soft lips thinned. One thing having money did teach a girl was how to resist blackmail and intimidation. A sweet young thing with substantial capital was a prime target for every variety of con man and woman, and Linda's earliest experiences and lessons had included self-defense measures against such people. Perhaps, she thought, slipping her coat on briskly and reaching for her purse and gloves, I am silly or even stupid, but I'm not easily scared.

The idea that the threat was directed against her changed her attitude sharply. Linda was not worried about how to protect herself; she knew quite well how to do that, quite aside from the fact that she was certain no personal threat was intended. All she wanted was to be certain that the candy was an attempt to drive her away. Although she felt competent to take care of herself, Linda was not fool enough to think she could protect a frail old woman.

The first step was to get the travel plans under way. Linda tossed the car keys up and down in her hand for a moment, then put them decisively in her pocket. A car was a nuisance in central London. There was never any place to park. She would have more freedom and make better time on the underground, and Mrs. Bates had said she could take a cab. She wouldn't need to do that unless American Express failed her and she actually had to go to the offices of the shipping line.

At the travel desk of American Express in the Haymarket, Linda stated her needs. Mrs. Bates was a clever old lady, but she *was* an old lady. She still thought of making travel arrangements directly with shipping lines and railroads. Linda knew she might have to tie up the final details herself, but there was no reason to run from one railroad and shipping line to another when a good travel agent would have most of the information, or would be better able to collect it for her. Linda took the time to explain in detail that the party she was escorting was elderly, accustomed to luxury, and one had a bad heart. There must be time enough between transfers to rest, to calm anxieties and explain away confusion.

The next step—while some poor clerk at American Express struggled with steamship and railroad schedules—was to phone General Barthemeles and find out whether he would be free that day. If he was, Linda intended to see him at once; if he was out or busy, she intended to make an appointment to talk to him as soon as possible. The general, fortunately for Linda's peace of mind, was at home. Although he was a trifle surprised to hear from her so soon, he seemed delighted to be called upon.

"In a snag already?" he asked jocularly.

"Yes, I am, sir, but not about the travel arrangements. Something has happened that frightened me very much. May I—"

"Emmeline frightened you?" the general asked sharply.

"No, no. Not Mrs. Bates. May I come and tell you about it, sir? I can't think what else to do."

"Certainly. Come along right now. I'll give you lunch and do my best to help."

Linda's sense of relief was enormous. There was security in the very sound of General Barthemeles's voice. She found when she had

been welcomed and divested of her coat, that
she was able to describe the entire incident,
from first noticing the gift-wrapped candy box
to Mrs. Bates's explanation, without faltering
or choking up. Aside from a question or two,
General Barthemeles did not interrupt. At first
his expression was of puzzlement, but that gave
way, as she told him her guess that someone
was trying to frighten her enough to leave Mrs.
Bates's service, to doubt shaded somewhat by
anger.

"Should I go to the police?" Linda asked finally. "That's what has been troubling me from
the beginning. It's all very well to guess I was
the indirect target—and if so, I don't care. I
don't scare easily and I can take care of myself
now that I know what to expect. But if someone meant to harm Mrs. Bates—that's a horse
of a different color. She—well, she isn't very
strong, I would guess. I couldn't accept that
responsibility."

"Don't see how the police could help," the
general said slowly. "Emmeline is stubborn as
an army mule. If she says she will handle this
herself, nothing will change her mind. And if
she won't cooperate and won't tell Gertrude to
cooperate, there's nothing the police can do."

Linda sighed with relief. She had been growing more and more reluctant to tell what might
well be considered a fantastic and unsubstan-
tiated story to the police. Her reluctance was
so great that she had begun to doubt her own
motives, so she was very glad to have General

Barthemeles reject the idea.

"If not the police, what should I do?" she asked, then smiled ruefully and added, "If you are willing to advise me."

The old man's white brows pulled together. "I'm willing enough," he began and broke off to utter a brief bark of laughter. "Always was one to stick my neck out. Wonder I never got m'head chopped off." He sobered and frowned again. "Trouble is, don't know what advice to give. Put your finger right on the point. Makes all the difference in the world whether that box was meant for you or for Emmeline."

"Does Mrs. Bates eat candy?" Linda asked. "I've only known her for a week, you see. I haven't any idea whether she does cheat about sweets."

"Used to—eat 'em, I mean, not cheat. Remember sending her some special kind from America once—pralines they were—" His voice checked suddenly. "But that was thirty years ago. Now . . . hmmm . . . I'm gettin' old. Sometimes thirty years ago is clearer than yesterday."

He mused in silence and Linda began to wonder whether he had slipped into a dream of the past. Just as she was about to say something to rouse him, however, he turned to her.

"Been thinkin'. Haven't seen Emmeline take a piece of candy since she was ill. Started usin' those little pills then—the saccharine—too. Strong willed, Emmeline is. No, she wouldn't have eaten it."

"But would everyone know that?"

"Ha! There you have it. Don't think so. Had to think about it a bit m'self. And her nephew and niece don't know her that well. Ah . . . there . . . was an estrangement. Only met Harriet and her children a couple of years ago m'self."

Linda hesitated, then said, "Yes, I heard. I'm afraid I've been listening to Gertrude gossip."

The general laughed his staccato laugh again. "Natural curiosity. All right. But don't take Gertrude as gospel. Peter might know, I think. Studies his aunt."

That was the last thing Linda wanted to hear. "But why should Peter want to be rid of me?"

General Barthemeles's thick white brows rose. "Don't think he does. Spoke very well of you. Wanted someone older at first but saw he was wrong. Nice thing about Peter. Always willin' to acknowledge when he makes a mistake. Can count him out. Fond of his aunt. Too fond, maybe. Drives her wild."

Linda could not help smiling. She felt much better. But then she sighed. "But the Sothebys don't even know me. They couldn't, surely, want to drive me away."

The old man's fine face suddenly looked drawn, and his lips set while he searched Linda's face. "Wish I knew you better," he muttered.

Linda shook her head. "I can't help you there, sir. I can assure you I'm trustworthy and discreet—but what could that mean? Even if I gave you references, it would be a while—unless you wanted to phone—before you could get answers. And, then, I would only give names of people who would say what I wanted."

General Barthemeles smiled slowly. "Smart gel. True, of course. And I'm used to making snap decisions about people. In fact, I didn't hesitate because I didn't trust you. Don't like to say things about people. If I hadn't been sure about you, m'gel, I would never have believed that wild story you came in here with—and I do believe it. Rose-Anne and Donald now—nice enough in their way, but spoiled. Harriet's one fault is that she'll do anything for those children." He shook his head. "They're jealous, you see. Jealous of Peter. Might think you were worming your way into Emmeline's affections—well, wouldn't have to worm much. Clear as paint she's already attached to you. But still seems a bit far-fetched."

"It does seem far-fetched," Linda agreed, "but the whole thing gets crazier and crazier the more I think about it. Maybe I'm making a mountain out of a molehill. Maybe there was nothing wrong with the candy. The incident is so—so purposeless."

"There was something in the candy all right," the general said. "I can't see Emmeline gettin' rid of it without a real reason. Lunacy—" His voice checked as if a shocking idea had come to him, but then went on steadily. "No. Just because we don't see the purpose don't mean there isn't one."

After a short pause for consideration, Linda said, "But we can't really do anything at all—

unless you think I should quit."

"No!" The negative was explosive, but then the general seemed to remember that Linda was not one of his troops. "At least," he added, "not unless you're frightened, m'dear. You aren't really much of a threat, and if someone acted against you, the motive for action is growing stronger. The next move would be a more dangerous one, and not against you."

Suddenly Linda's mouth felt dry. She understood all too well. If she quit and removed herself as a diversion, the next move might be against Peter, and it might be a real attempt at murder instead of a gentle warning.

"Gertrude can be trusted to guard Emmeline like a lion," General Barthemeles continued, "and though you're quite right that Emmeline isn't strong, she's wide awake on all scores. Anyway, an army of police couldn't really protect her. But don't say you can't do anything. You can watch and listen with a far less prejudiced eye and ear than Gertrude's. And if you can spot the person"—the General's eyes were very keen and his jaw jutted forward—"I might find a method of settling things once and for all." He stood up. "Now, that's enough of that. Come and have lunch and tell me how you are making out with the travel arrangements."

Chapter Eight

By the time Linda left, full of excellent food served silently and efficiently by a man almost as old and just as well-preserved as the general, she felt quite cheerful. Her stop at the Haymarket did nothing to diminish her good mood. The long-suffering clerk provided her with a number of printed schedules and price lists and promised complete itineraries with alternative hotels, routes, and connections if she would return in a few days.

Having agreed, Linda moved on to the next step of her duties. She found a phone and a directory, called Handy Andy and arranged for a man to come and drag out the trunks, then an agency that rented electronic typewriters to have a machine delivered the next day. Then, out of sheer high spirits, she set out to walk to the nearest stationers to purchase tags for the trunks, typing paper, and carbons, in case she had to fill out shipping forms.

Linda found herself swinging along, whistling softly and happily. Her stride almost faltered as her conscious mind caught up to her unconscious reaction. Frightened and worried she had been and might be again, Linda realized, but since General Barthemeles had virtually cleared Peter—and certainly the general knew everyone involved very well— she was happy.

Unnatural creature that I am, Linda thought, trying to feel remorseful, *I don't care about anything except that the excitement is making me feel alive.* But no matter how she tried, Linda couldn't work up any remorse. No one had been hurt—and when emotion was replaced by logic it was clear there had been no intent to harm—and any threat there had been had been directed against her. And Peter Tattersall wasn't involved.

The fact that Peter's name had come into her mind twice in two consecutive thoughts did impinge on Linda's consciousness, but a stationery store loomed up just in time to save her from needing to examine the idea. Her purchases completed, a glance at her watch told Linda that if she did not hurry, the library Mrs. Bates favored would be closed. She almost trotted to the underground, thinking of little besides which books might be available. It might be best, under the circumstances, to forego mysteries for a while and stick to biography and romance.

Coming away from the library, which she had caught just as it was closing, Linda's mind was still on books. It seemed to her now that not taking any mysteries was a mistake. Perhaps the omission would be so glaring that it would arouse anxiety? Linda thought of going back, but knew it was too late. Finally she decided to tell Mrs. Bates, if she asked, that she felt nervous and reluctant to read a mystery. Linda was annoyed with herself and still somewhat preoccupied as she opened the door and walked up the stairs. Gertude's sudden appearance in the short corridor took her by surprise.

"Madam is in bed," the maid whispered.

"My God," Linda gasped. "What's wrong?"

"Nothing, nothing. Madam often takes an afternoon in bed on Monday—although I think what happened may have worried her more than she lets on. Mr. Peter is in the kitchen. He wants to talk to you."

Linda felt her expression change, made a desperate effort, and, she hoped, concealed the spurt of pleasure she felt. She started forward, but Gertrude caught her arm.

"I had to tell him, Miss Linda. In spite of what madam said, I was that upset, I couldn't sleep a wink last night."

Linda smiled. "That's all right, Gertrude. I would have told him myself, but I didn't know where to reach him. I couldn't ask you because last night you seemed dead set against telling anyone."

"Well, I'm not so sure I did right," Gertrude muttered. "He's that angry. He's fair wild! I didn't know what to say to him or how to calm him down. He was off to get Mrs. Bates's doctor to her, even though I told him and told him that she never touched a bite and that having the doctor would upset her more than anything else. I only stopped him by telling him to wait till you got back."

Gertrude's description of Peter's state seemed no exaggeration. As soon as Linda opened the door, he leapt to his feet and came forward, his brows drawn in a furious frown.

"Have you agreed to this lunacy too?" he roared.

"Oh, Mr. Peter," Gertrude hissed, shutting the door tight, "keep your voice down, do! She'll hear! You don't want her more upset, do you?"

With a visible effort, Peter lowered his voice. "Did you agree not to have a doctor look at Gert and to just let my aunt go her merry way?"

"I suppose I did," Linda said slowly, "but I don't think you need to worry about your aunt, and Gertrude made Gert promise to get a checkup today. Please sit down, Peter," she said as he made an impatient movement toward the door. She sat at the table herself, and after a moment he did too. "You really should hear what your aunt said to me, and I assure you she was under no strain this morning. Her breathing was even and her color was good. She—she almost seemed to be enjoying some little private joke." Her lips tightened as his expression changed to a mixture of contempt and sympathy.

"I very nearly went to the police," she said.

"Good God, no!" Peter exclaimed.

"You see, I don't know any of you very well. I wasn't afraid of losing my job—that's not why I didn't call a doctor or go to the police. I just wanted to do what would be best, and General Barthemeles agreed that—"

"General Bar—How the hell does he come into this?"

Linda swallowed. "I had to talk to someone, someone who knew you all well. I couldn't— Well, you've been so worried about how your aunt would react that you don't seem to realize that to me it looked like an attempt at murder."

"Murd—" Peter's face went white. Then he shook his head violently. "No. No. I can't believe it."

"Your aunt doesn't think so either. I told you she called it a piece of mischief. I couldn't accept what she said, but I started to think—"

"And you went to the general instead of to me? You think I tried to kill Aunt Em?"

Linda found that her thoat had closed. She could not force out a word. There was a breath-held silence, but what showed in Peter's eyes was pain, not fear or rage.

"No," Linda burst out in a gasp. "I never believed that. But I didn't *want* to believe you could be involved, so I couldn't trust myself. Don't you see?"

There was another silence, but it was very different. The hurt was gone from Peter's eyes, and a slow grin of mingled shyness and triumph spread across his face. He reached across the table and took Linda's hand. She made no attempt to pull away, but did not smile in return.

"I was so desperate at first that I would have called you—only I don't know where you live or work."

An expression of total amazement was followed by one of real pleasure on Peter's face. All he said, however, and that rather dryly was, "There are telephone books, you know."

"Yes, but by the time I thought of that, I also had time to examine my own motives— and they were not exactly pure," Linda replied, equally dryly. "I didn't want to believe you could have done it," she went on seriously, "but you had the opportunity—everyone except General Barthemeles had the opportunity."

"What do you mean? How can you know that?"

"By accident, but I'm absolutely sure of it. Listen, and you'll see I'm right. When lunch was announced, the general went out first with your aunt and Mrs. Sotheby. Then Donald, Rose-Anne, and you, in that order. I stayed just a moment to empty the ashtrays. You know your aunt can't abide the odor of stale smoke. When I was looking for dirty ashtrays, I looked at every flat surface in the drawing room—and there was no box of candy. There were briefcases and two folded newspapers that could have covered the box, but it wasn't in the open."

"I see," Peter muttered. "I see."

"Not yet, you don't. Not the whole thing. When I got to the dining room, everyone was there, but Mrs. Sotheby was just getting up to leave and you, Rose-Anne, and Donald were sitting like mummies. Mrs. Sotheby came back a minute or two after I sat down, and after waiting for someone else to be civilized, I started to make small-talk."

Peter looked a trifle conscience-stricken. "I guess Rose-Anne got to me. Sometimes she does. She has a damn good eye for a weakness, and she said something that made me lose my temper."

"Not the most stable in the world," Linda said, grinning at him. "It was fairly obvious. Anyway, I was happy as a clam with the topic I chose at the moment, but like a clam I couldn't see far enough. You see, Donald and Rose-Anne both went out to get papers to show me. And then"—Linda's voice took on a note of exasperation—"you had to be noble and get your own coffee, so you went out too."

"In fact, the only one except my aunt who didn't leave the dining room was the general." Peter looked at Linda with marked admiration. "My God, girl, you've got brains!" But the expression of pleasure disappeared as quickly as it came. "And if you had brains enough to see that, you should have had brains enough to get a doctor over here to look at my aunt and Gert."

"We've been through that. Besides, I wasn't worried about Mrs. Bates. She didn't touch the candy—" Linda hesitated and frowned. "The box wasn't sealed in any way. It had a big satin bow around it, but that only fit into the cover. But I know she didn't take even one piece because they were all there. You know those fitted plastic shells with round and oval and square holes to fit the candy—every space was filled."

Peter drew a long breath. "All right. But if Aunt Em doesn't eat candy—and she isn't foolish about things like that—at least, I'm pretty sure she doesn't . . . does she sneak sweets, Gertrude?"

The maid had been listening to them silently, looking more and more worried. "No, she doesn't, Mr. Peter. And I clean her room and go through her drawers all the time. I've never found anything hidden."

"Then obviously the candy wasn't meant for Mrs. Bates," Linda said slowly and distinctly. "It was meant for me."

"Nonsense!" Peter exclaimed, but his face went white. "Linda, that's crazy. No one could possibly want to hurt you."

"No one does want to hurt me," Linda assured him. "There wasn't enough of anything in that candy to hurt a healthy young woman. Gert had four pieces, and she's smaller and lighter than I am, and she was only sleepy for about an hour. I probably could have eaten the whole box without getting sick. It was an attempt to scare me off, I think."

"Oh," Peter said slowly, grinning again. "So that's why you thought I might be involved. I take back my remark about your brains. Of course, I'm glad you realized I wasn't trying to poison my aunt, but you aren't very perceptive if you believed I don't want you around."

"It's no joke, Mr. Peter," Gertrude put in sharply. "Madam must have guessed that too, and she shouldn't be worried."

"She must have guessed," Linda agreed, and then told Peter the gist of his aunt's conversation with her. "That's the main reason I didn't go to the police," she concluded. "The general agreed with me and pointed out that if Mrs. Bates refused to press a complaint—even if she could press one now that the candy is gone—the police couldn't act anyway."

A Delicate Balance

But Peter didn't seem to be listening. He was staring at Linda's hand, which he still held. Quite suddenly, he got up and put his arm around her. She could feel that he was trembling very slightly.

"It isn't a joke," he said, his voice now tight and strained. "A person who's crazy enough to take a chance like that—What if you were a greedy little thing and did eat the whole box at once? Will the fact that this didn't work—however it was meant to work—increase the pressure? Will . . ." He hesitated and then went on in a rush. "Will the person take crazier and crazier chances? And one of them might hurt you, Linda. You'd better quit."

"No!" Gertrude and Linda exclaimed simultaneously.

Linda said no more and bit her lip. She couldn't offer the general's reason—that Peter would be endangered if she left her job—and she couldn't think of another really good reason to stay. Fortunately, Gertrude had one all ready.

"You can't quit, Miss Linda, you can't. I'll watch out for you. I swear it. You won't eat anything that doesn't come direct from my hand, and I won't let you be alone with any of them. I'll watch. Madam has taken to you so much. She hasn't been so bright and cheerful since—for a long time. If you quit, she'll fret and fret over it, worrying about what she did to make you go. Mr. Peter,

123

don't you dare tell Miss Linda to quit."

"I don't care whether he tells me to or not," Linda said, smiling. "I'm not going to quit, so long as my staying doesn't endanger Mrs. Bates." Peter tightened his grip on her and she looked up at him. "Don't you worry about me, Peter. I've been traveling around alone for quite a while. I know how to take care of myself."

"A stud is one thing; this is another," Peter growled. For a moment he looked as if he were about to say something else, but he didn't, and after a moment he released Linda and returned to his seat. "Well, that tears it," he said after a short pause. "I hadn't intended to come out to Corfu this year. We're busier than a three-legged dog with an itch and I can't really afford to take more time off, but—" He sighed. "But I'm not going to see you take that trip alone or wander around that barn of a house with no protection. You'd better reserve for me as well as for Rose-Anne and Donald."

Linda thought briefly of protesting that the general would be there and repeating that she could take care of herself, but she didn't. For one thing, she doubted Peter would pay any more attention to what she said this time than he had previously; for another, she was too eager for Peter's company to suggest the sacrifice. His employer would just have to manage without him since, from the way he spoke, there didn't seem to be any danger that taking the time off would cost him his job.

"Where do you work?" she asked. "In case something turns up and I have to get in touch with you."

"Bates Engineering," he replied briefly, then gave her his home phone number and his number and extension at the office. "Don't ask for me by name," he said. "Just give the operator that extension. If you ask by name, you'll have to wait for a year."

So I was right, Linda thought as she noted down the numbers, he does work for his aunt's company, and I'm sure he won't lose his job no matter how much time he takes off. It must be a large firm, too. But that was no surprise; Linda had always assumed the late Mr. Bates's business had been successful because Mrs. Bates seemed to be very well off.

Linda was a little sorry that her guess about Peter's dependence on his aunt had been confirmed. She would have preferred that he had obtained a job independently— but that was a foolish notion. No doubt he made a better salary and had more freedom working for his uncle's company. Also, his aunt might have insisted he work for her husband's firm if it was a family concern, as many English companies were. Since Mrs. Bates had no children and neither Donald nor Rose-Anne would be interested in employment in an engineering firm, Peter was all the family there was.

When he saw that Linda had written down the phone number and extension, Peter said, "Now, if anything happens, you call me. Don't go running around to outsiders and, for God's sake, don't go to the police or try to take care of it yourself."

Linda looked up under her lashes. "Yes, master," she intoned with spurious meekness. Peter sputtered, but Linda did not follow up on the joke. She looked at him soberly and shook her head. "I will let you know, of course," she said, "but I'm going to tell General Barthemeles too. For one thing, it would look odd to him if, after being in such a flap, I suddenly had nothing else to say. Besides, he'll be with me all the time I travel, and I trust him."

Peter's eyebrows shot up. "Meaning you still don't trust me?"

"Yes, I do," Linda replied softly. Then she lifted her eyes to his defiantly. "The trouble is, there really isn't any reason to trust you." The shadow of an arm across an ill-lit stairwell was a shadow on Linda's heart. "And I want to trust you so much that I don't dare trust myself."

Chapter Nine

If Linda had had to wait for another incident before speaking to Peter privately, she wouldn't have gotten to know him any better in the next few weeks. However he was only clumsy physically; he was adept enough at social relations. Before he left Mrs. Bates's apartment that Monday afternoon, Peter had convinced Linda to check with him daily by phone. He didn't wish to call her, he explained, because no matter what either of them said, Mrs. Bates would be sure he was checking on her and would be annoyed.

In the course of shopping and making travel and shipping arrangements, Linda spent a good deal of time out of the house, and part of that time was in Peter's company. He often "happened to be free" for lunch when she was or "in the neighborhood" when she was scheduled to see the travel agent. Linda was scarcely innocent enough to be taken in by these coincidences, but she was equally unlikely to put a stop to events that flattered her and that she enjoyed.

Linda was getting a double thrill. She was attracted by Peter as a man, but she was also aware that his interest in her was specially valuable because it could not possibly have even the smallest mercenary taint. It was remarkable, Linda thought, how stimulating it was to know you were attractive when you were *not* a good catch.

Since Linda did not undervalue herself, she had never felt the young men who dated her were *principally* interested in her money. She had been told often enough by people who did not want to marry her that she was an attractive girl with a sweet, cheerful disposition. Moreover, since most of the young men she knew were no more poverty-stricken than herself and had no need for a rich wife, to see her income as their principal interest in her would have been paranoid. But her invested capital certainly did not detract from her appeal either. No doubt it even added a certain charm—young men with money are far more aware of the value of a wife with a good income than most others.

Peter, of course, knew her as a girl who had to work to live, and his interest in her, therefore, must be based solely on her personal attraction. Unless, a small insistent voice hissed, the charm is in your position with Mrs. Bates. But Linda wouldn't listen to the snake's hiss of suspicion that threatened to mar her pleasure. It was a stupid suspicion. Peter had a much closer and more influential ally in Gertrude. Besides, he showed not the slightest interest in his aunt's doings when he was with Linda. If she told him something, he listened, but he never questioned her about Mrs. Bates.

Linda was less convinced that it was her personal charm that drew Donald's attentions. To her surprise, he had called her on the Tuesday after the Sunday they met. His excuse was to be sure she had been willing to make their travel arrangements. He had been far politer than Rose-Anne, had even half-laughingly apologized for his sister's manner. But when Linda assured him, truthfully, that she would make their reservations and, mendaciously, that she had not been offended by Rose-Anne, he was in no hurry to hang up. He had thanked her for smoothing over the awkward hump in the conversation at Sunday's lunch and then asked whether she was really interested in the production end of television.

Linda wondered whether he was so desperate to separate her from Mrs. Bates that he was thinking of offering her a job at the television studio, but she merely assured him that she found the subject fascinating. Whereupon Donald promptly invited her to come and see the "works" first-hand. Whatever his ulterior motive, Linda was pleased. She agreed without hesitation that she would be delighted to come and promptly arranged to meet him on her day off.

The visit was a success. If Donald had an ulterior motive, it didn't show. He spent about two hours enthusiastically showing Linda the workings of his department, from casting lists to continuity charts. Fortunately, the studios were at a distance from the offices so that the slight anxiety Linda had felt about running into someone who knew her came to nothing. Donald did offer to take her over and show her the actual recording of a show, but he was rather flattered when she said she wasn't interested in that part.

He had arranged the visit for the late afternoon, and by the time he was done explaining, it was time for dinner. Linda suspected when he asked her to stay and dine with him that the BBC tour had been a form of buttering her up. Now, she thought, he'll ask for payment.

Once again she was wrong. The conversation remained as general and pleasant as it had been before. In fact, Donald's one moment of awkwardness was when he had to explain that he couldn't see her home personally because he had to return to work. Linda laughed at him, assuring him she didn't mind taking the underground. She was unlikely to become prey to muggers at eight-thirty. He would not hear of that, however, and put her into a prepaid cab, telling her that he had seldom enjoyed an afternoon and evening more. His final words were a request for permission to phone again and make an appointment for a proper dinner-date.

Linda had to conclude that there was no immediate favor or benefit Donald wanted and knew, too, that he *had* enjoyed her company. She had enjoyed his. Yet, when he called on Friday to ask whether she could come dancing with him Saturday night, Linda approached Mrs. Bates to ask her permission without a qualm. Her strongest emotion was curiosity. Would Mrs. Bates disapprove? If so, would it be because she was jealous, as elderly people sometimes were of the attention their relatives paid to others, or would it be because she felt her nephew should not date her employee?

Mrs. Bates, however, did not disapprove. She seemed delighted, if surprised. The surprise was easily explained: "I didn't think Donald had good enough sense to appreciate you, Linda," she said wryly.

In fact, Mrs. Bates was so pleased and entered into Linda's preparations for her date with so much enthusiasm that Linda couldn't help wondering whether there was a little malice in the older woman's pleasure. Did Mrs. Bates know that Mrs. Sotheby would disapprove of Donald dating her sister-in-law's companion?

Mothers often wanted their sons to marry well, and a childless woman sometimes nourished a deep-hidden spite against a woman who had had children. If so, Mrs. Bates might be likely to encourage a relationship that Mrs. Sotheby would dislike but that would not harm her nephew.

Linda was not in the least troubled by either notion. She liked Donald. She would be happy to go out with him whenever he asked her, but she was indifferent to Mrs. Sotheby's displeasure (if she would disapprove) and to Mrs. Bates's malice (if there was malice). Neither could affect her because she did not expect to become seriously involved with Donald.

That was odd. He was handsome (much better looking than Peter), intelligent, and, when he wanted to be, charming. A brief consideration of her reaction to him gave Linda the answer and made her laugh. Of course. Donald was exactly like all the young men she had dated all her life—courteous, suave, and worldly. He probably would never roar at her in a temper. On the other hand, he would probably never impulsively embrace her in front of a maid. Nor would she be able to read every emotion as it passed nakedly over his face.

Once she had made the comparison, Linda was troubled. It came to her mind that she had never told Mrs. Bates how often she met Peter outside the house. In fact, she never mentioned meeting him at all. She had taken no chances on Mrs. Bates forbidding those meetings. Linda had half realized that she liked Peter better than any other man she knew, but when she found herself comparing others to him and finding them less satisfactory—that was dangerous.

Dangerous . . . What a peculiar word to use. How could there be any danger in falling in love with Peter? Irritably, she pushed the idea away. There was danger in falling in love with anybody.

Life became quite a whirl. There were lunches with Peter, dinners with Donald, appointments with shipping clerks and travel agents, shopping for Mrs. Bates, herself, and Gertrude, packing and labeling, as well as the ordinary duties of answering the mail, helping with entertaining, and reading to Mrs. Bates. Linda fell into bed each night, asleep before her head touched the pillow. She was too busy to realize that she had not been bored for a moment in several weeks. She was certainly too busy to worry about drugged boxes of candy and shadows on a stairwell. The last night Linda spent in her bed in Mrs. Bates's apartment, she was so tired she never finished buttoning her pajamas.

By the time Linda closed the door to Mrs. Bates's compartment on the night ferry-train from London to Paris, she felt as if she had been spinning at high speed while careening drunkenly from one spot to another like an ill-guided whip top. A long sigh trickled out of her, and she leaned back against the windows of the narrow train passage. A deep male chuckle brought her head around sharply.

"Thought you'd never make it, didn't you, m'dear?" the general asked, his voice lowered to a growl that the clackety-clack of the train would cover.

"I never would have made it without you," Linda replied gratefully.

"Well, maybe not," he agreed with a second chuckle. "Come and have a drink with me and catch your breath."

A drink! Linda sighed again, this time with pleasure. She certainly needed a drink. And she didn't feel in the least guilty about needing one, she realized. She deserved a drink!

As they settled into comfortable chairs in the club car, Linda's mind passed over the events of the past few hours. She sputtered, trying to hold back a giggle, and then gave up and laughed aloud.

The general had given their order. Now he looked at her and, in a moment, he was laughing, too. "Plenty of uses for an orderly room voice, even out of the army," he chortled.

"Yes," Linda gasped, wiping away tears of mirth. "Oh, yes." She shook her head. "I did think that three hours was enough time to get from Mrs. Bates's house to the train—I mean, even with traffic, it's only a twenty-minute drive. But I knew we'd had it when Mrs. Sotheby announced that her white overnight case had been left in the cab. I knew it hadn't been. She didn't have it with her. I assure you, I know the size and appearance of every single piece of luggage we have. I can even tell you how many nicks and scratches each piece has."

General Barthemeles cleared his throat explosively and snorted. "I knew Harriet would take it, but I wasn't sure of Emmeline. In fact, Emmeline doesn't usually fuss that way. I started to think she *wanted* to miss the train, maybe that she didn't want to make the trip at all. Has she said anything like that to you?"

"No." Linda felt surprised. "She seemed very eager to leave whenever we talked about it, but I've been so busy. . . ."

"Mmm-hmmm. That may be it. She remarked to me that Peter hasn't been around much recently. Maybe with your time taken up— Oh ho, so that's it, is it?"

Linda had felt herself blush when Peter's name was mentioned and, foolishly, had looked away, making it easier for General Barthemeles's keen eye to catch the betraying color. "Peter and I have had lunch together a number of times," she said defensively. "But I don't think he's visited his aunt less often. Well, of course, he hasn't been to lunch, but he stops in almost every day after work."

"And Emmeline always complained about Peter's comin' to lunch. I know. But old people are unreasonable, m'dear. They can't stand the noise the young 'uns make, but feel neglected when they don't show up."

"Not you, sir."

"Oh, yes. I'm just as bad as Emmeline." A fierce frown wrinkled the old man's brow and, under the bristling moustaches, his mouth twisted wryly. "Why do you think I decided to come along with Emmeline? My son doesn't choose to pay his usual visit this year, so—"

"Well, sir, all I can say," Linda interrupted, smiling, "is that I'm profoundly grateful to him. I couldn't have managed without you, sir. You must know that." A dreadful thought crossed her mind, and Linda's eyes grew round with apprehension. "He won't change his mind, will he? I mean, you won't go dashing home and leave me to cope?"

The general's booming laugh made the other occupants of the car look up, but he didn't notice. He took Linda's hand. "No, m'dear," he said warmly. "I won't leave you. In fact, Richard did me a good turn. . . ." He hesitated, then went on briskly. "I'll see him in the spring, or perhaps he'd like to bring the children out to Corfu." He paused, staring at Linda but clearly not seeing her. "Hmmm. Yes. That might be a good idea. I understand that Emmeline's house is quite large. When Peter, Donald, and Rose-Anne have gone home—if Harriet will stay—hmm. Yes. That might work out very well."

Linda could not see what Mrs. Sotheby's staying on had to do with the general's son, but she was delighted that General Barthemeles seemed to be diverted from whatever unpleasant idea of being unwanted had been disturbing him. She sipped her drink peacefully as he mused, allowing the alcohol to warm and relax her, allowing her mind to slip back to yesterday.

Both Peter and Donald had said very warm goodbyes. Indeed, it was the first time Donald had shown a sign of any emotion beyond friendliness. Linda hoped that the two weeks' separation (they were to spend time in Paris, Florence, Rome, and Naples before boarding the ship for Corfu) would return him to normal. If he showed any deepening interest in her, Linda knew she would have to find some polite way of turning him off.

Peter was another matter. There had never been the smallest doubt in Linda's mind about what kind of interest Peter had in her. But Peter . . . Linda shook her head and straightened up in her seat. She simply was not going to think about Peter. It always made her feel like a bright sunny day with an ominous ring of black clouds just below the horizon where you couldn't see them but they could rush out and soak you through in moments.

One worry pushed out another, so Linda's next thought was of the steps she had taken to avoid trouble at their stopovers. Probably even if Mrs. Bates and Mrs. Sotheby did any sightseeing they wouldn't go places where Linda's friends were likely to congregate. And Linda had almost driven the travel agent into a breakdown by refusing one first-class hotel after another. She gave various excuses—one was too modern, a second too noisy, a third too crowded—but the true reason for her rejections was that her jet-set friends frequented those hotels. Eventually, dignified, old-fashioned places that Linda felt would not appeal to her crowd were found. Now all she had to worry about were chance meetings in shops or restaurants.

Linda gave an absent-minded "yes" to the General's question about another drink and considered expedients. "Do you think Mrs. Bates and Mrs. Sotheby will do much shopping in Paris?" she asked.

General Barthemeles's laugh boomed again. "I can assure you that Harriet will," he replied. "She has a list as long as your arm from Rose-Anne. And Emmeline hasn't been to Paris for years—not since poor Edward got sick."

"I hope I'll be able to get them into the shops early, before they get crowded," Linda said.

"Shouldn't think you'll have any trouble there. Old folk don't sleep all that long and, in a strange bed, I shouldn't think all that well. They'll be glad to be out early."

"And I hope to be able to convince Mrs. Bates to rest in the afternoon," Linda mused, half to herself.

"Yes, indeed," General Barthemeles agreed with rather surprising heartiness. "It would be an excellent idea for Emmeline to rest in the afternoon."

"Then we could have dinner, either at the hotel or—I'll have to check with Mrs. Bates to find out whether she has some favorite place she'd like to eat so I can make reservations." Linda took out a little pocket diary, which used to be sparsely filled and now was densely overwritten and found a spot to make a note. Then, quite suddenly, she yawned. She covered her mouth and gasped, "Oh, excuse me."

The General smiled kindly. "No, no, m'dear. I know it's the effort, not the company. Off you go to your compartment. Sleep well."

Over the next week, Linda did manage to avoid meeting her old friends, although disaster was only narrowly averted twice: once when Mrs. Bates chose to shop at the same modiste favored by Ethel Levy and again in Maxim's where Joseph Sarnov was having an early pre-theater snack when Linda's party was having dinner. Linda escaped recognition, but her heart was pounding and her hands were clammy with anxiety each time.

On the train to Florence, Linda was less exhausted. Mrs. Sotheby seemed either cowed or reassured by General Barthemeles. He had only to say firmly, "You did not forget it, Harriet. It is with the luggage and Linda has checked on that," to reduce her to quiescence. Linda was not sure it was a happy quiescence and she spoke hesitantly about it to the general, but he merely replied she should leave Harriet to him. Mrs. Bates, now that the initial move had been made, showed herself not to be a dither-er. She did insist on checking everything with Linda, but once checked, she remembered.

Relaxed over a drink—alone this time but grateful to the general for initiating the custom—Linda had time to wonder why she felt that recognition by her friends would have been a disaster. First, was she ashamed of her position? That is, was she trying to hide what she was doing from her friends? A giggle escaped her as soon as she thought of it. She would love to tell them; love to see their horrified or uncomprehending faces. No, it wasn't that. Suddenly she felt bleak. She had realized that she didn't care what any of them thought; she didn't care if she never saw any of them again. In fact, she didn't have any friends.

Linda saw clearly that it was what she was doing that she was trying to protect. It was Mrs. Bates, not the friends of her past life, whom she didn't wish to shock. Yet now she felt much less anxiety about getting another job. She would do well, she thought, in a travel agency. Still . . . The thought of Peter intruded and Linda pushed it firmly out of her mind. Why should being fired by Mrs. Bates interfere with her relationship with Peter? Presumably it was not a heinous crime to be bored and believe doing an honest job would cure it, and being well off did not ordinarily cool a young man's pursuit. No, she could explain to Peter. It was something else.

The daiquiri Linda was sipping so slowly tasted delicious, yet she knew it was not as well made as many she had drunk in the past. Her mind wandered to their arrival in Florence, to the need for packing three elderly travelers into one cab and herself, Gertrude, and the luggage into another, to organizing the suites at the hotel. She had the answer to why she was so eager to keep her job in the delight that filled her as she planned expedients. She realized she had never enjoyed herself so much in her life as during the past few weeks when she had all the burden of planning, fitting schedules together, and arranging for others to do the chores she couldn't carry out personally in such a way that they couldn't make mistakes.

The drink tasted good because she was satisfied with herself. Linda's eyes widened and she sat up straight, a pleased smile curving her lips. Why, she was a born organizer! The hell with jet-setting and a worm's eye view of life. She was going to run something, build it into something big. What?

Garbage, she thought. Garbage was really interesting. There was too much garbage everywhere and reusing some and disposing of the rest was a complex problem—and organized crime was mixed up in garbage too. That should certainly add to the excitement. It wasn't a grab-it-this-minute-or-lose-it sort of enterprise either. There was plenty of time to investigate and decide just what she wanted to do. One thing was sure; the garbage wouldn't go away no matter how long it took.

Another thing, she couldn't just drop Mrs. Bates. She had taken the job, and until Mrs. Bates decided she didn't need her or Linda could find an adequate substitute, she would keep on doing the job. But it was a big, wide, wonderful world—and it was all her oyster. All she had to do was crack it open and extract the meat. Linda finished the last sip of her drink, rose to her feet, and stretched luxuriously. She had come a long way from the sobbing girl on Claridges' sofa. There was obviously something to be said for the Puritan ethic of hard work.

Chapter Ten

Florence and Rome were safely negotiated. Linda went to the airport to meet Donald, Rose-Anne, and Peter and discovered that Peter had missed the plane. Fortunately, he had managed to have Rose-Anne paged at the airport before she boarded and tell her which flight he expected to make. Linda sent Rose-Anne and Donald ahead in a cab, leaving the car she had rented in the parking area, and settled down to wait.

Donald had urged her to leave Peter to get to the hotel as best he could. Cabs, after all, were plentiful.

"I would just love to," Linda snapped with sincere irritation, "but he doesn't know where we're staying because we had to shift hotels. And, frankly, I don't trust the system here to get a message to him."

With a chagrined laugh, Donald admitted this was so. "Do you want me to wait for him?" he asked.

It was a considerate offer, and Linda hesitated a moment before refusing. In that moment reason mastered her irritation with Peter and she shook her head. "I wish I could," she said, "but I don't think Mrs. Bates would like it and, besides, you've been traveling and must be tired. In a way it's better." Linda glanced at the piles of luggage that had come off the plane labeled with Rose-Anne's name. "We'd never fit all the bags in the Alfa I rented, so one of us would have had to go in a cab with the luggage anyway."

By the time Peter arrived, Linda's good humor had been completely restored. She was actually looking forward to having a little while alone with him. He was obviously delighted to see her, waving vigorously and grinning all over his face.

As soon as he was in earshot, the grin turned wicked. "My bet paid off," he said with a broad wink. "Did you send Donald and Rose-Anne on ahead?"

"Do you mean you missed that plane on purpose?" Linda gasped, torn between laughter and exasperation.

"Of course." The crooked, boyish grin that was so endearing broadened even further. "And I missed this one too—didn't I?"

"What?" Linda exclaimed.

"Yep. Missed this one too, just by a hair. Had

to phone the airport long distance and leave a message to say that I was taking the plane to Rome and would drive the rest of the way."

For ten seconds, Linda gaped at him. Finally she drew a long breath, held it for a moment, and then, helplessly, burst out laughing. "Is there one to Rome at the right time?"

"I'm not such an idiot as to forget to cheek that. It leaves only fifteen minutes later and arrives at the same time this one did, but it would take me time to rent a car and to drive— at least two hours, even on the autostrada—so we have two whole hours to ourselves."

"But Peter," Linda sputtered, "we're going to spend two weeks together, living in the same house."

Peter's smiled turned wry. "My, you are an innocent, aren't you? Aunt Em wouldn't just look cross-eyed if I started sneaking into corners with you. Don't be a fool, Linda. We can be friendly and pleasant when my aunt's around, but no more. If I showed how I really felt about you, Aunt Em—well, I'm not sure whether she'd tell me to leave or fire you, but it would be one or the other."

"I don't think that's true, Peter," Linda said, but her voice was uncertain. "When Donald asked me out to dinner, your aunt was pleased."

The grin disappeared from Peter's face, and his eyes narrowed. Linda felt frightened. The clumsy, boyish, appealing young man she knew had suddenly changed into a hard-faced stranger.

145

"Playing the field, aren't you?" he snarled.

"Yes, I am," Linda snapped defiantly. "You don't own me. And I think maybe you did make this plane after all. The car is in the lot just across the way. We can leave right now, and you won't have to pretend a thing for your aunt."

"Hey, wait a minute," Peter exclaimed, catching at Linda's arm as she started to walk away. "God, what a spitfire. You don't have to blow your stack just because I'm a little jealous. Most women take that as a compliment."

But it hadn't sounded like jealousy to Linda. It had sounded far nastier, carrying an innuendo of hired companion trying to make a security deal with either one of her wealthy employer's nephews. Yet what right did she have to be angry, Linda thought, biting back a furious retort. Her behavior did rather look like that. She hadn't told Peter about her dates with Donald, and he couldn't know that financial security was the last thing about which she needed to worry. So all she said was, "Please let go of my arm."

"Linda," Peter said softly, "I'm sorry. At least have a drink with me. I'm tired and—and maybe I did think—or hope that I owned you. No, that's—that isn't what I mean. Oh, damn it all, you know what I mean."

"Do I?" To her chagrin, Linda felt tears rising. She could feel them hanging in her lower lids and she struggled to prevent more from coming so they wouldn't spill over.

Linda was as shocked and surprised by her

sudden tearfulness as Peter, who uttered a stran-
gled, "Oh, my God," and dropped his bag so he
could put both arms around her. It was scarcely
the place for an avowal of faith or even for comforting a young woman whose feelings had been
hurt, as Peter realized. After a hearty squeeze,
he pushed Linda away and grabbed his valise
as suddenly as he had dropped it.

"Let's get out of here," he muttered.

What had astonished Linda so much that she
had failed to react when Peter grabbed her was
the tell-tale tears. They had brought a final reali-
zation of the true depth of her feelings. It was
far too late to consider that falling in love was
dangerous. It was far, far too late to tell herself
that Donald was handsomer and had better
manners than Peter. It was equally useless to
question or berate herself about why. She was
head over heels in love with this man—a man
who grabbed her in public, then pushed her
away, who made nasty innuendos about her
character and purposes, who said he thought
he owned her.

The enormity of that idea stunned Linda further so that she let herself be herded, with shoves
from Peter's shoulder and elbow, out of the airport building and right to the parking lot. Still
numb, she took the lead to the car. By the
trunk, Peter held out his hand and she put the
keys into it, in the next moment finding herself
firmly escorted to the passenger's seat. At the
exit, she heard the liquid flow of Italian, and
money changed hands.

Somehow Linda had expected Peter to be as clumsy with foreign languages and customs as he was in moving. Her mouth felt dry and she glanced sidelong at him as he wove through the traffic. When he exited the highway, she made an effort to speak, but nothing came out, and she swallowed hard. It was impossible—impossible to be in love with a man of whom she knew so little. What *had* they talked about during all those lunches? Yet if at that moment Peter had said, "Marry me," Linda would meekly have put her hand into his and followed wherever he led.

It was neither church nor temple that Peter led Linda into, however, merely a large roadside cafe. He did not stop at the tables sheltered under umbrellas, gay even in the failing light, but urged Linda on ahead of him into a dim room and steered her toward a booth in the back that was, to her unadjusted eyes, as dark as pitch.

"Look," Peter said, after having shoved her somewhat ungently into the booth. "I better say this loud and clear and make my explanation later. I love you. I've loved you since you made your first nasty crack at me that day I met you in Aunt Em's sitting room. I thought I made it pretty clear even if I never said the words. It's hard to find a time to say those particular words at lunch. You have no idea how hard it is. I tried and tried to find a place to put them in between the appetizer and the soup or between—"

"Peter!" Linda choked. "I'll murder you! Between the appetizer and the soup, indeed! How dare you make me cry one minute and laugh the next."

Peter groaned. "Don't tell me you're one of those women who goes to the movies and says 'I enjoyed myself so much—I cried and cried.' If you prefer crying to laughing, I'm going to take it all back."

"If you can take it back, I don't want it!" Linda snapped, simultaneously outraged and laughing.

Peter's face sobered with terrible suddenness. "I wish I could take it back. God, I love you, Linda. I'd like to get a special license and marry you this minute—and I don't know when I can ask you to marry me. And I wish I didn't love you."

This time Linda felt no urge to weep or rage. The shock that had brought tears was over and the depth of emotion with which Peter spoke was too great to waken anger.

"Why?" she asked softly.

"Because of Aunt Em. Linda, she's a very sick woman, and she's my only living relative. I can't and won't do anything to upset her."

Although her eyes had adjusted and the corner was no longer so dark, Linda suddenly felt chilled. "I'm sorry," she said. "I don't see the connection between Mrs. Bates and us. And she doesn't look or act like a sick woman."

"No. She doesn't even know. I thought of telling you sooner. I guess I did tell you a little when you were first hired. The doctor felt that anxiety would be worse for her than ignorance.

That's why I wanted a nurse disguised as a companion for her, but she took to you so warmly that . . . Linda, you must realize I couldn't take you away from her."

Linda blinked. "But Peter, surely you didn't expect me to stay forever? It's only a job. Why your aunt might live ten or fifteen years. Did you expect me to live with her—"

"My aunt won't live one year," he said, his voice harsh.

Linda's corner seemed to darken again and get colder. "I can't believe that," she whispered. "I've seen people with heart disease. They have swollen legs and blue lips. They can't breathe."

"That's coronary insufficiency or congestive heart failure. My aunt doesn't have that kind of heart disease. She's got an aneurysm they can't operate on—maybe more than one. One day it will . . . burst." His voice broke, and he swallowed. Then he added, "When you get back to London, you can speak to her doctor yourself."

"If she's that ill, she must have a doctor in Corfu," Linda said. She wouldn't, couldn't believe that Peter was making this up or exaggerating his aunt's illness, but her throat closed when she saw his face go cold and hard.

"Yes, she does, a half-baked quack recommended by that fool, Mrs. Paxton." He shook his head. "Maybe he isn't so bad, but he doesn't have the equipment. In any event, there isn't much any doctor can do, so he's as good as another. In a way it's better that he doesn't think there's anything more wrong with Aunt Em than growing old."

"If there's nothing anyone can do, Peter, let's not talk about it. Let's forget the whole thing. It's cold and dark in here. Let's go outside."

Linda hardly recognized her voice. It was thin and high with fright. Peter's eyes, which had been fixed into the distance over her shoulder, came back to her face.

"Oh, honey, I'm sorry. I didn't mean to scare you. I'm a damned fool. I only wanted to explain why we couldn't get married."

Linda's breath eased out. Peter's every emotion played so openly across his face—anger, worry, fear, love. He was not a fool; he could handle her like a virtuoso. But there was no guile in him, no deceit. Whether or not Mrs. Bates was ill, Peter sincerely believed she was. Perhaps the London doctor was playing on his fears. Mrs. Bates was a private patient, one who paid her doctor herself rather than being included under the government program.

Linda's opinion of the medical profession was not high. She knew far too many doctors who pandered to "nervous" young women and "exhausted" young men, who prescribed drugs and gave "treatments" more for the purpose of fattening a wallet than restoring health. No doubt it would be a great temptation to an English doctor whose income was limited by government-set allowances to make Mrs. Bates's condition seem more serious than it was. Or perhaps the Corfu doctor's diagnosis was inaccurate.

Whichever doctor was right, Peter feared the worst because he loved his aunt. Linda remembered when Uncle Abe had had a simple hernia and she had been terrified. She had been sure it was cancer, convinced that the doctor and Aunt Evelyn were lying to her so that she would not worry. Linda shook her head, more at herself than at Peter.

He had started to say something, checked it at her negative gesture, and then burst out, "But I can't drop it, Linda. Damn it all, whatever my citizenship I'm not a patient Englishman. I'm a brash American—and I love you."

His voice had become so loud that Linda put a hand over his. "Yes, that's lovely, but don't tell the whole of Italy."

Peter was usually quick to see a joke, but this time he didn't laugh. "Maybe it's funny to you, but it's not to me. Don't you see where that leaves me? Am I going to have to sit around and hope that my aunt will drop dead so I can get at you?"

The words that should have sent Linda deeper into the dark of doubt lightened her spirits instead. It was so open, so innocent a statement of frustration, that she smiled.

"Don't you care at all?" he roared.

The bellow brought the dilatory Italian waiter scurrying across the floor. "Signori?" he asked anxiously.

Peter looked up at the waiter, his lips drawn

back from his teeth. The man stepped back, and Peter shook his head, his expression returning to normal. "*Niente*," he said. "*Perdone*." His hand brought out his wallet, and he slipped a bill into the man's hand. "This was a mistake," he said to Linda. "Can we talk in the car?"

"All right," she agreed, sliding out of the booth, "but I hope you don't plan to bellow at me with the windows closed. My head will ring for a week."

"No," Peter said, taking her elbow, "I don't plan to bellow at you."

There was such an odd sound in his voice that Linda's head lifted sharply, but he had turned toward the car as they stepped out the door and all she could see was the side of his face. The lights around the outdoor tables picked out the quiver of a small muscle in the cheek near his mouth. That made her suspect he was amused, but he had opened the car door and gestured for her to get in before she could ask and she thought better of posing the question as they drove away.

They did not drive far; perhaps four kilometers down the road Peter turned into a rough track and bumped about fifty feet off the road. He doused the brights, turned off the engine and turned to face her, his mouth a hard gash and his eyes only black hollows in the faint light from the dashboard. As he moved out from under the steering wheel toward her, Linda suddenly felt frightened, but the arm he stretched out went gently around her shoulders and when he bent forward, it was to kiss her.

For a few heartbeats the touch of his lips was tentative, but as the tension went out of Linda's body, he kissed her harder. The hand he had left resting on the steering wheel, as if to allow her an open space to twist away from him if she wished, now grasped her upper arm, then slid up so that the fingers were touching her cheekbone and ear. He stroked, oh so gently. Linda shivered, and let her lips part, and after a moment let her head fall back on the support of his arm.

"I told you I wouldn't yell at you," he murmured.

Linda chuckled deep in her throat, but found she could not answer, even though his mouth had freed her lips to nibble her chin and travel lower with feathery little kisses along her throat to the little hollow where the pulse beat, faster and harder than usual. Her hands had been still, gently folded in her lap, but as Peter's mouth moved sideways toward her ear and his hand slid down to her breast, she raised one of hers to his head and laid the other on his thigh, then moved it between his thighs. She stroked. Peter groaned.

The sound usually associated with anguish did not discourage Linda at all. She was a small-town girl raised with small-town values despite her money, but she had lived on her own from the time she had gone to college and, between the money and the fact that she was piquantly pretty, she had plenty of experience with men.

A Delicate Balance

She slid her hand deeper and felt Peter's hips lift in response as he groaned again.

Her touch had not paralyzed him, however; in fact one pleasure seemed to generate the need for others. Linda discovered that Peter's hands, hopelessly clumsy in large movements, were apparently as agile as his mind in minute maneuvers. With totally unexpected skill, he had undone the buttons of her blouse, slid her strap down, and insinuated his fingers into her bra. She shivered again as the fingers soothed her breast and his thumb, light as a whisper, tickled her nipple.

Linda was not a virgin. She had yielded to pleas and skilled seduction when she was younger and had briefly thought herself in love, but her consent had been more owing to what she believed a person in love should feel than to the demands of her body. Now, suddenly, she wanted what she had accepted, enjoyed, but never actively needed before.

The hand with which she had been stroking Peter's hair dropped quickly to his belt. Fingers made clever by urgency found the metal pin and popped it out of the belt hole. The leather slid free of the buckle as Linda manipulated the button of his trousers through the buttonhole and slid the zipper down. Peter gasped, buried his head in her neck, lifted it and seized on her lips, then dropped his head to kiss her neck again, his hand feverishly stroking her breast. He was breathing as if he were running hard, and suddenly he pulled the arm with which he had been supporting her shoulders down between her and the seat to her hips, lifted them, and with surprising strength pulled her toward and under him while he tried to raise himself and move back.

Disaster struck immediately. Unprepared as she was for the change of position, Linda's head slammed against the window ledge of the door, and her legs, unable to follow her hips, banged against the seat. Peter's rear hit the steering wheel with such force that he was propelled forward onto Linda, slamming her head, which she had unwisely lifted, down on the ledge again.

There was one moment of absolute silence, then Peter, very faintly, said "Dammit." And then, louder, "Are you all right?"

Fortunately the ledge of the door was padded vinyl, and Linda had been far more surprised than hurt. "Yes," she replied, in a rather choked voice. "The ledge is nice and soft."

With some care, Peter lifted himself off her and wriggled back under the steering wheel. As she also slid back and got upright, Linda could sense him closing his trousers and belt. She shrugged her bra strap up and closed her blouse, not knowing whether she was going to cry or whoop with laughter.

After a moment she swallowed hard. "I'm afraid we'll have to think our maneuvers out more carefully if we want to go on with this," she said.

"Go on!" Peter shouted, turning toward her abruptly and promptly banging the knee of one long leg against the bottom of the dashboard. "God damn it!" he bellowed, "I never intended to start! I'm too old to make love in cars! Especially one this size."

"Yes, dear," Linda agreed with spurious meekness, "but considering how you made me feel, I think you're too tall rather than too old."

Peter made a sound, starting with a growl that ended in a choke of laughter. Then he sighed. "But it isn't funny," he said. "You've got to know I'm half out of my head to grab you like that. All I wanted to do was put my arm around you and try to make you understand why it's so important to me not to upset my aunt."

Linda said, "Peter, you've got yourself worked into a lather about nothing—"

"Maybe because it isn't nothing to *me*," he interrupted, turning his head away to stare out into the dark.

"Peter! Shut up and let me finish what I want to say."

"But Gertrude's right about Aunt Em," he interrupted again. "If you quit, she'll fret herself sick over why. And how the hell could I marry you if she—"

"Peter!" Linda exclaimed, her voice tight with exasperation. "Stop dramatizing yourself and the situation. You're a big boy now. The world is not black and white. There are lots of ways to work this out."

"I don't see one, and I've been mulling this over and over, turning it round and round—"

"That's why you don't see anything. Of course

we can't get married tomorrow—"

"Then you will? Oh, Linda—"

He leaned over to take her in his arms, but Linda braced her hands against his chest and pushed back and he dropped his arms. "If this was all a big act to stampede me into agreeing to marry you, Peter Tattersall, I'm going to kill you, not marry you. Besides, you haven't asked me yet."

"No, it wasn't—well, yes, maybe a little. But not the part about Aunt Em. Anyway, will you marry me as soon as—God damn! What kind of a proposal is that?"

Joy, pain, and eagerness were so mixed in Peter's face and voice that Linda was torn between a need to comfort and a need to laugh. She compromised by smiling and saying softly, "I will marry you, Peter, as soon as we can be married without endangering your aunt's health."

"That's wonderful! Linda, you're wonderful! What an idiot I am. Why didn't I ask you sooner instead of—But I couldn't believe you'd understand, that you'd be willing to put up with such an indefinite, long-range thing."

"It won't be as long-range as all that," Linda stated dryly. "And I hope it's not all that indefinite."

One thing Linda was sure she was going to organize before thinking about garbage was Peter. He might know where he was going and even how to get there, but Linda was positive the same goal could have been achieved with much less wear and tear on both of them.

"I didn't mean that kind of indefinite," Peter said indignantly, and then after a short pause, "Do you see a light at the end of the tunnel, Linda? I want you, but I want Aunt Em too. I want—" He reached toward her again, jerked away, and started the engine of the car with a vicious twist of the key. "We'd better get back to the hotel. If we stay out here in the dark, I'm going to drag you out into the nearest ditch."

Linda bit her lip, determined not to laugh. How she could love Peter so much and not feel a single impulse toward a full moon, violins, and sweet music or candlelit intimacy was amazing. It wasn't that she didn't want to touch Peter, to kiss him, to make love—she certainly did, even after the fiasco they had been through. She wanted him so much that all the fancy extras weren't necessary. With Peter she would enjoy making love on a subway platform—provided they were alone. She didn't need the tinsel trappings of romance.

"If you'd told me," she said, with only the faintest quiver in her voice, "I'd have brought a blanket."

Peter choked. "Efficiency expert," he said. There was a faint bitterness in his voice, but the tension of frustration eased.

For a few minutes Peter gave all his attention to backing the car out of the farm track. Neither spoke again until they were safely back on the main road, but when they turned toward the city and their hotel, Peter sighed heavily.

Roberta Gellis

"This is going to be one hell of a vacation," he remarked bitterly. "Maybe I just better get a call from the office before we get on the boat and go back. I'll be a mental case seeing you all the time and—and I'd have to watch you play games with Donald. No. I can't do it."

"Your aunt would be heartbroken, Peter. She's been looking forward to this boat trip and having 'her children' all together in the house. And she misses you. She talks about 'when Peter comes' all the time."

His expression softened. "Okay," he sighed. "If that's what Aunt Em wants—" But then his lips thinned. "But you stay away from Donald."

Linda almost offered a quick assurance that Donald was not in the least necessary to her, but instead she smiled mischievously. "No, I won't. Don't be so silly, Peter. If I go walking with Donald, I can also go walking with you—or swimming or dancing. In fact, it would be most unnatural if I treated you two differently."

First Peter started to smile; then his mouth grew sour again. Linda watched sidelong, amused at the ease with which she could read his thoughts. She might not be able to "manage" Peter, but she always knew exactly where she was with him.

Chapter Eleven

It sounded easy: if Donald opened one door, Peter would open the other; if Donald seated Linda, Peter would pull her chair back. Unfortunately, theory and practice were as far apart as usual. For one thing, Peter was so clumsy that Donald had opened doors, moved chairs, and generally been attentive before Peter had got done bumping into the furniture. For another, Rose-Anne could not be ignored in favor of Linda. And, along that line, it was reasonable that Rose-Anne should prefer the attentions of an unrelated male to those of her brother.

The pairing-off was natural, Linda told herself, but she was somehow uneasy, even though she caught anguished glances from Peter now and again. When she was with Peter, she was aware only of her response to him; when they were separated, her brain began to function again. Originally she had thought about the events and conversation of the afternoon to relive her pleasure, but as she replayed them, a number of odd facts stood out.

For example, how did the reversal of their positions on the subject of secrecy come about? Peter had started by insisting they conceal their relationship from his aunt. Before the afternoon was over, it was Linda who was insisting on secrecy and Peter who was complaining about the need for it.

Looked at from one angle, his reversal was natural. He had raised a problem he wanted to be talked out of and instead Linda had agreed with him. Still, the turnabout made Linda uncomfortable. Had she somehow been maneuvered into the position? Was Peter's seemingly naked emotion only playacting?

The following afternoon, Linda still had not answered either question and was still pushing them out of her mind frequently. She had just returned her attention to the packed luggage in Mrs. Bates's room when a pair of strong arms went around her and a man's beard scratched her face while his lips were pressed to her throat.

"Ulp!" Linda exclaimed unromantically.

"Hmmm. Good. I've been wanting to do that all day."

"Peter! Your aunt—"

"Is downstairs in the lobby having a cuppa. I was sent up to remind you that the blue dressing case is to go into my aunt's stateroom, not with the large valises."

Linda turned in Peter's arms, gave him an enthusiastic but brief kiss, and shoved him away emphatically. "None of that, now," she said with mock severity. "Stop acting as if this were a Victorian melodrama and you a wicked lord kissing the housemaid. You know I—" Her voice checked abruptly, and she turned her head.

"I know you what?"

"That's funny," Linda said, not answering Peter's question or his grin. "I thought I heard the door open and close. Maybe it was the bellboy for the luggage. Go and catch him if you can, Peter."

While she waited, Linda opened the bathroom door and checked in the medicine cabinet and on the shelves to be sure that nothing except hotel property remained. She was opening and closing every drawer in the night stand, bureau, and dresser when Peter returned with the boy. Once again, she counted the bags. All correct in number and appearance.

"Do you have a luggage truck?" she asked.

"Perdone?"

Linda hesitated, mentally arranging her stumbling Italian, but Peter translated for her.

"Si, signorina, avero," the boy replied.

Linda took the blue case in her hand and gestured toward the other bags. *"Prender questi, per favore, e veniere,"* she said to the boy, who began to carry bags out and load them on the cart. "Was he heading for Mrs. Sotheby's room?"

she asked Peter idly as they waited. Instead of answering as indifferently as she had asked, Peter hesitated, making Linda look at him questioningly.

"You must have been mistaken about hearing the door," he said, looking away awkwardly. "The boy was just coming out of the elevator when I got down the hall."

So someone was spying on them, Linda thought. She didn't really care because Peter was certainly innocent, beyond his reluctance to betray one of his relatives' sneaky behavior. And his effort at concealment was transparent enough. So she made no comment on his statement, merely remarking that she had to check Mrs. Sotheby's and the general's rooms. Peter came along and, when all the luggage had been collected, accompanied her down to the lobby where Mrs. Bates's party was whiling away the time before they left for the ship by having tea.

In the lobby Linda and Peter parted. Linda went to the desk to arrange about cabs to take them to the ship. When she was finished, she joined the tea party, setting down Mrs. Bates's blue and Mrs. Sotheby's white dressing cases, which she had been carrying.

"Oh," Mrs. Sotheby said, as soon as her eyes fell on the case, "my hand lotion. I forgot to pack it."

"It's packed, Mrs. Sotheby," Linda said positively. "I checked the medicine cabinet, the undersink cabinet, the shelves and all the drawers."

"Are you sure it's packed?" she twittered.

Linda handed over the case, which was promptly opened and inspected. Mrs. Sotheby uttered a soft wail. "It isn't here. I knew I hadn't packed it, and it's my special kind that the doctor prescribes. Oh, Linda, you must have overlooked it."

"Not in your room, I didn't," Linda replied, but she put down the cup of tea she had poured for herself and added with resignation, "I'll go up and look again, just to be sure."

"No, that's no use. Oh, I don't mean you wouldn't look, Linda, but you wouldn't see it. You've made up your mind that it isn't there, and even if you want to find it—I'm not explaining myself very well," she faltered as Mrs. Bates's eyebrows went up. "It's like proofreading what you've typed yourself. Rose-Anne is always telling me that she reads what she *thinks* she typed, and she never sees her own mistakes."

Linda, who had been a bit annoyed at what she felt was an unjust accusation of carelessness and stubbornness began to laugh. "You know, Mrs. Sotheby, that's perfectly true," she admitted. "Probably now I wouldn't see that bottle even if it grew legs and followed me around the room."

"Ugh, what a revolting thought!" Donald exclaimed.

"No it isn't." Peter chuckled. "I can just see that bottle—on very short legs, running with a decided waddle because, you know, bottles don't

165

bend in the middle—following Linda anxiously, maybe wagging its—"

"Peter!" Mrs. Bates cut him off. "Control your imagination. We aren't getting any closer to Harriet's hand lotion. Perhaps you'd better go up yourself."

"No, Emmeline, there's no use in sending Peter or Donald. Men never see things. Rose-Anne, dear, would you—"

"That's enough." The general's boom silenced not only Mrs. Sotheby but everyone in the immediate area. "If Linda says the lotion is not in your room, Harriet, it is not. We have been traveling for two weeks, and not once has any object been left in hotels or cabs. If the bottle of lotion is not in your dressing case, then it is in one of the valises."

There was a momentary silence. Mrs. Sothby did not look startled, frightened, or offended, which did not surprise Linda, who had been through similar scenes before. Mrs. Sotheby's brow creased in thought. Then she smiled.

"Why, I do believe you're right, Cecil. Now I remember. I wrapped the lotion in my night gloves because I use them together so it seemed logical that they should be packed together." She turned to Linda. "I'm sorry, my dear. It's true enough. You never forget anything."

Linda murmured some suitable reply, but her attention was mainly on Rose-Anne, who was staring at the general with astonishment. Her eyes went to her mother, then returned to the general. All she had said was, "I'm glad I don't have to take off on that wild goose chase," but her expression was thoughtful, and a glimmer of light began to flicker in Linda's brain. Mrs. Sotheby and the general—well, why not? He had lost his wife and was lonely. He was the kind of man who was accustomed to looking after people. Mrs. Sotheby was also alone; her children lived with her, but they might not mind having the place to themselves. And Mrs. Sotheby seemed to welcome being looked after.

Although Mrs. Bates was also alone, she was much older than Mrs. Sotheby. Aside from that, Mrs. Bates did not need to be protected and guided and would, in fact did, resent any efforts in that direction. Peter's efforts to care for his aunt certainly exasperated her.

The train of thought brought Linda's eyes to Mrs. Bates. She recognized clearly for the first time that her employer was a dominating woman. Linda looked down at her cup and lifted it. She was ready to swear that Mrs. Bates's feeling for General Barthemeles was no more than friendship, but she was not at all ready to swear Mrs. Bates would relish the idea that he could feel more than friendship for any other woman. There was nothing in Mrs. Bates's expression to indicate that Rose-Anne's behavior had any special meaning for her. Nonetheless, Linda was moved to look at her watch and remark that the cabs would be waiting in about fifteen minutes.

The reminder started enough movement to cover the awkward revelation—if there had been one. Rose-Anne went to make a last check on her twin's room and her own, Peter went out to see to the loading of the luggage, and Linda nibbled a cake and finished her cup of tea. She wondered where Gertrude was, but didn't bother to ask. Somehow, Gertrude was always standing right beside the vehicle carrying the luggage when it was time to leave.

"You are sure you have the tickets, Linda?"

"Right here, Mrs. Bates," Linda replied, smiling and pulling a corner of the packet out of her purse so it could be seen.

"I should have saved myself the breath for asking. Really, Linda, you have made this trip so easy and pleasant. What I always hated and what finally made me stop taking trains was chasing all along them in the wake of a porter who didn't know where you belonged any better than you did. How do you always know which car we are in?"

"By running down and looking at the train the day before," Linda confessed, laughing. "Didn't you notice how I disappeared for an hour just about departure time the previous day?"

Mrs. Bates laughed aloud at Linda's exposure of her methods. Then she sighed. "Well, that can't work for the ship. I suppose we'll be caught in that awful crush of people waiting for a steward."

"Oh, no, ma'am, I'm smarter than that," Linda protested. "I wrote to the line and got a plan of the ship." She pulled this from her purse and spread it on the low table in front of them.

"Now, we enter here, at gangplank A. We cross the inner deck, turn left, and take the elevator up to the top level. Then we go left again until we come to the central cross corridor, and your suite is right there—A4. I can see you and Gertrude inside and then go back to take care of arrangements with the Purser."

General Barthemeles, who was as well acquainted with the ship's plan as Linda, leaned forward and put a heavy finger on Suite A4. "Hmm. Yes. Well, here you are, Harriet, one deck down in a double cabin with Rose-Anne, and Peter and Donald will be sharing this double farther along but on the inside. They'll change with you if looking at the sea bothers you."

"And where will you be, Cecil?" Mrs. Bates asked, peering interestedly at the plan.

"Another deck down. Decided I'd rather be alone in a less rarified area than tripling with those two youngsters. Better for them—plenty of pretty young things aboard—and better for me. Don't want to be waked up when they stagger in in the small hours." He paused and chortled throatily. "Besides, Linda's right next to me in C17. I know when I have a good thing."

Linda looked at her watch. "I think it's time, Mrs. Bates, Mrs. Sotheby."

A born organizer, Linda thought as she laughed silently at her reflection in the mirror of her tiny cabin. Everything had gone like clockwork. Even Rose-Anne and Donald

169

had been wafted aboard the *Helena* without an unnecessary motion or a single complaint. Peter—Linda giggled—well, of course, he had nearly fallen into the water, but even perfect organization can meet its match, and Peter was a match for anything.

Linda fluffed her hair with her comb, pulled the ruffles at her wrists free, and smoothed her hands across the rose-colored skirt that clung to her hips and then swept to the floor in graceful folds. When she turned to lay the comb down, her knee brushed the narrow bunk bed and her outstretched hand nearly touched the wall. The little cabin was nothing like the suite Mrs. Bates had, nor much like her own usual luxurious accommodations. Linda could not deny that she now looked forward to regaining that luxury, but for the time being she was content to have her privacy. Gertrude had obviously thought Linda was mad when she said she would prefer this single, tourist-class cabin to having Mrs. Bates get a larger suite and sharing that. But Gertrude did not plan to dance away the nights and walk the moonlit decks after Mrs. Bates was alseep.

Content with what she saw in the mirror and her plans, Linda took the elevator up and knocked at the door of Mrs. Bates's sitting room. Gertrude opened it and smiled at her.

"My, you look nice, Miss. Is that a new skirt?"

"Yes, shhh," Linda whispered conspiratorially. "I was extravagant in Paris. I bought two blouses and another skirt."

"Just as well. You'll find you have to dress for dinner every night aboard ship and three or four times a week in Corfu."

"But why aren't you dressed, Gertrude? I know you sit at our table."

Linda was troubled. Gertrude had said nothing to her about where she usually ate when she traveled with Mrs. Bates, and Linda had assumed she would eat with the family. In fact, Mrs. Bates had approved the plan.

"Yes, Miss, but madam is a little tired tonight. We'll dine here together."

"Is she asleep? Shall I stay, too?" Linda asked, hoping she didn't look as disappointed as she felt.

"There's no need for that, Miss. But madam isn't sleeping. You can go in and talk to her."

Linda found Mrs. Bates sitting up in bed propped by pillows. She did not look particularly tired, but Linda thought she was breathing a little faster than usual. She did not ask how the older woman felt because she had noticed that Mrs. Bates really did not like that. To her inquiry as to whether she should stay, Mrs. Bates laughed gaily.

"You are a good girl to ask, Linda, but I couldn't be such a monster. Here you are all dressed up, and you look delightfully pretty, too, and looking forward to a dinner-dance, I'm sure. No, you go and enjoy yourself."

"Shall I come and read to you after dinner, Mrs. Bates? I brought along several books." Linda felt obligated to make the offer, but she hoped Mrs. Bates would refuse, and that hope was fulfilled.

"Not tonight, my dear. I think I'll go to sleep early. You just enjoy yourself."

And enjoy herself Linda did. Donald danced like a dream and Peter—well, he shouldn't have danced at all, but Linda didn't mind getting her toes stepped on if she could be in Peter's arms. There were other young men, too, and whenever Linda returned to the table everyone was in the best of good spirits and on best behavior. Linda even danced with the general, a staid foxtrot, although now that it had been brought to her attention she noticed how very much his interest was centered on Mrs. Sotheby.

Linda danced until the last strains of "Good Night Sweetheart" signalled the end of the party. To avoid recriminations, she refused all offers to escort her to her cabin, even from a young man who pursued her out onto the deck. He was so young and so hopeful, however, that Linda stood talking for a few minutes before she refused him again and moved away. Although she should have been dropping with fatigue, Linda knew she would not be able to sleep immediately and did not want to return to her cramped stateroom at once. The night was only refreshingly chilly, so she clambered down an external companionway and set off with a swinging stride to walk off her excitement.

As Linda turned the curve of the ship's body, it seemed to her that she heard a faint clang from the metal stairs. It made no particular impression on her. Others were leaving the ball-room and almost certainly some would choose to walk along the promenade decks. Actually, what drew Linda's attention was the fact that there were no sounds of footsteps. She glanced over her shoulder casually as she walked, then stopped and peered. Was that a shadow moving?

Her first impulse was to wait for whoever it was to catch up. Then she smiled to herself and started off again. Probably it was that silly boy, and she certainly didn't wish to encourage him by waiting. She moved on briskly, breathing deeply and looking out at the horizon where the stars seemed to lie almost in the sea. When it was clear that no one was following her, she stopped and stood by the rail for a while. Now her feet ached a bit, and she could feel the muscles of her calves and thighs quiver with tiredness.

Much more slowly now, Linda made her way to another companionway and went down to her own deck level. She had lost her orientation and was not sure where her cabin was, so she moved close to the inner wall to see the numbers of the passages. To her chagrin, she found she was on the opposite side of the ship. Linda paused. It was, of course, possible to walk across through the passageway. That would shorten the distance but—she looked out at the dark sea again—it was such a lovely night. Better to put a cap of beauty on it. Smiling and humming "Good Night Sweetheart" to herself, Linda strolled along the deck.

Perhaps it was the fact that she was humming that masked any sound, Linda thought later. And certainly it was the carelessness of the deck steward, who for some reason had failed to fold and stack the chairs in one section, that made her aware of the movement. Staring intently to keep from bumping anything, Linda saw something move—a shadow in shadow, it flitted from near the rail to the deeper shadow near the inner wall.

It could have been someone out for a breath of air, but the movement was so furtive that Linda's heart began to pound. She turned toward where she thought the shadow had disappeared, straining her eyes. Was there movement? Was a darker blot within the darkness coming closer?

Suddenly a scraping sound behind her, near the rail, made Linda whirl, catching her breath. She backed up slightly, stiff with terror as another blot of shadow began to grow. Between the two, she was trapped. Even as she watched the thing by the rail swell larger and larger, she was aware of movement along the wall, creeping steadily toward her.

Out of the hunched, rising thing, a thin shadow stretched upward. Linda could feel a scream rising in her throat, strangling her, but not a sound came from her parted lips. The thin thing wavered, groped—

"God damn!" Peter's voice said thickly. "God damn!"

Chapter Twelve

"Peter!" Linda cried, moving toward him.

Relief mixed with a new fear slowed her; it seemed like minutes before she reached him. Just as she was about to put her arms around him to help him up—for he was on his knees with one hand clinging to the rail—she heard a deck chair scritch along the planking. Her head whipped around, but only in time to see the door of the passageway close. Someone had been hiding in the shadows along the ship's side, someone who had slipped into the corridor. That was no innocent bystander out for a breath of air. With a soft cry, Linda went down on her knees beside Peter.

"What happened?"

He was rubbing his head with the hand that was not clinging to the rail. "Someone tried to push me overboard," he muttered. "No. I don't believe it. I don't. I—"

"Peter, can you stand up?"

"Just a minute. I caught my head a crack on the rail, I think, and everything's on a merry-go-round."

Linda's first impulse was to run for help, but she discarded the notion as fast as it came to her. She couldn't leave Peter alone. Although she had heard the door of the passage close, there was no guarantee that whoever had assaulted Peter was not waiting there, hoping to catch him in a weakened condition. The idea made Linda look nervously over her shoulder at the door, but the light behind the glass remained unshadowed. Linda also thanked God she had come along just then. She did not want to think about what might have happened if she had walked a little slower or watched the stars a few minutes longer.

Fortunately, before she could frighten herself any more, Peter pulled himself erect. He seemed to waver, then steadied. "I'm all right," he said. "I was only dazed for a minute."

He stretched out a hand and Linda, who had risen with him, caught and held it. "Come to my cabin," she urged. "I'll call the ship's doctor."

"Don't need him."

"If you hit your head hard enough to be dazed, you do need a doctor. Oh, Peter, did you hit your head, or—" She couldn't finish that thought and left the words hanging.

"Of course I hit my head. There was no *or*

about it. I must have put a foot wrong and slipped."

His eyes shifted as Linda simply stared. She had been frightened; now she was angry. "I don't mind covering for your family when someone does a peeping-tom act, especially when there wasn't anything to see, but attempted murder is a little different."

Peter's eyes came back, challenging, and he said harshly, "There wasn't anyone here with me. When I slipped, I must have felt as if there had been a blow on my back—or maybe I'm sensitive about being so clumsy. I was alone. Who could have pushed me?"

"You weren't alone. I saw someone moving in the shadows. And when I ran over to you, whoever it was slipped into the passage. I didn't see the person, but I saw the door close."

Peter continued to stare down at her, but Linda knew he couldn't see the expression on her face because her back was to the light, and she had deliberately kept her voice flat. After a moment he turned his head and looked out at the quiet sea.

"The ship's movement might have shut the door, and the way the light shifts might have made you think you saw someone. I say there was no one here. What could you prove? Let it be, Linda. I'll be careful. Nothing will come of it."

He spoke so quietly, with such sad resignation, that Linda found herself repressing tears. Peter was too, she thought, although his voice was steady, only a little huskier than usual.

"You know who did it," she whispered.

Again a long pause. Then, "Yes, if anyone did anything."

"And Mrs. Bates said she knew who left the candy. Was it the same person?"

This time the pause was shorter. In the faint light from the doorway, Linda saw Peter's hands clench briefly on the rail. Then, suddenly, he uttered a choked laugh. "What a woman!" he muttered. "Yes, it was the same person, but—"

"This was a joke too?" Linda barely got the words out. She wasn't sure whether she was more frightened, more incredulous, or more furious.

"A joke?" Peter repeated slowly. "Yes, Aunt Em did tell you it was a joke. Well, I don't think it's a joke, exactly, but I don't think it's dangerous either."

"It's not dangerous to have a maniac that plays homicidal games loose in the family?" Linda's voice was now light and pleasant. She was beginning to feel the whole situation was totally unreal. In the aftermath of the double shock of the attempt on Peter and his determination to shield the attacker, Linda felt detached.

As if her question had wiped out his last doubts, Peter began to laugh. "No, it isn't dangerous. Really it isn't. Oh, come on, Linda, look at the height of the rail. I'm a big man. A shove couldn't push me over. Someone would have to grab me by the feet and lift to toss me overboard. And you yourself admitted that the candy stunt couldn't have hurt anyone."

"You didn't think being pushed was funny at first." Linda was beginning to feel doubtful herself. Looking at the rail behind Peter, she had to admit that there was very little chance a push could have tipped him overboard.

"Maybe not at first," Peter responded quickly and more soberly, "but that was partly because of the crack on the head and partly because—believe it or not—my feelings were hurt."

"Your *feelings* were hurt?" Linda's voice scaled upward.

She shook her head and stared around, wondering whether she would see the White Rabbit and the Mad Hatter or the Cheshire Cat's smile. She certainly felt as if she were at the lunatic tea party in *Alice in Wonderland*.

"I know it sounds funny," Peter said apologetically, "but what I mean is I never felt really threatened—only hurt. I—I guess I didn't want to believe that sh—that anyone felt that way about me."

"And now that you know someone would like to kill you, you don't think it's important?" Linda spoke clearly and rather slowly, as if to a feebleminded child.

"Important?" he repeated, his voice sad again. "Yes, it's important, but not for the reason you think. I'm not in any danger." He turned suddenly with the jerky swiftness so characteristic of his movements and snatched Linda into his arms. "Linda—Linda, darling, do you love me?"

The question was so urgent and intense that

Linda hugged him back instinctively. She could feel his arms tremble as he held her. "Of course, Peter. Of course I love you."

"Thank God for that. If I didn't have you . . ." He kissed her long and hard, then thrust her away to arm's length, swallowed, and laughed uncertainly. "That's enough of that, or I'll end up in your cabin for the wrong reasons."

But Linda, although stirred by the kiss, was not about to lose sight of the real problem. "Peter, it's because I love you that I can't accept your casual attitude about this." Again she spoke slowly and quietly, feeling as if she were reasoning with a retarded child. "I'd like some assurance that you'll still be around when we *can* get married."

"I'll be around," he said confidently. "Look, Linda, try to understand. This small family is all I have. Mom and Dad and I moved around so much that I never put down roots, never made any real friends. Then Mom died, then Dad, and then I got the news that Uncle Ed—he and Aunt Em wrote and phoned all the time—was sick. So I came to England. But in England I didn't even have the casual acquaintances I had in America. My Aunt Em—" His voice shook. "Never mind, but these are all the people I have. I may fight with Rose-Anne and Donald, but—but they're my *cousins*, and Aunt Harriet is my *aunt*. I never had relatives before."

"But—"

He cut her off sharply. "There aren't any buts. I tell you, Linda, I wouldn't do anything to hurt any of them even if it *did* mean the risk of my life, and it doesn't. I assure you, I *swear* to you, I'm not in any danger."

After that it was impossible for Linda to press him. She could only insist that he come to her cabin—it didn't take much insisting to convince him to do that—so she could look at his head. And he had been right when he said the blow had been slight. Though he winced when Linda felt around, she couldn't even detect a lump.

Assured that he truly wasn't in any danger, Linda put aside her doubts and suspicions—at least temporarily. All the time she had been examining his head, Peter's hands had roamed over her back. Now she slid down on his lap, and their lips met. Evidence of his excitement was immediately obvious; Peter needed no more priming, but Linda had learned her lesson in the car the previous night. Her stateroom was very cramped, and she had no intention of permiting a slapstick bump and fall act to break their mood again. Before she allowed herself to surrender to the mounting pleasure Peter's lips and hands were generating, Linda had calculated how best to get him out of his clothes without getting a black eye.

She began by pulling her lips free and murmuring, "Take it off, lover. There isn't room in here for us both to wave our arms around."

He jerked to his feet, twisted his head to look at her, and began to say, "Are you s—" as his body turned. He broke off when their knees banged together painfully and yanked off his jacket, saying, "The hell with you being sure. I'm sure."

When he had his shirt off, Linda stood up right against him. His breath drew in hard, but he made no other movement when she undid his pants and pushed them down, catching the elastic band of his shorts in her thumbs so both garments came down at the same time. Then she put one finger against his chest and pushed. She didn't really exert any pressure, but Peter sat down on her bed as if his legs had crumpled. A minute later, Linda had his shoes and socks off and then his pants and shorts. She tossed those on the one chair and then bent over, offering Peter her mouth, murmuring just before their lips met, "Your turn."

Peter might look glassy-eyed, but there was nothing slow about his response. Mouth open to invite her tongue, his fingers undid the button of her waistband, slid the zipper down, let the skirt drop, and rid her of her panties. He stroked her buttocks, let his hands slide down the back of her thighs and pulled gently, first on one leg and then the other. Linda came atop him with one knee on each side of his narrow hips, but he did not maneuver to enter her, merely pulling her down against him so she was pressed hard against his shaft.

So excited that she was totally unaware that she still wore her blouse and camisole, Linda moved against him seeking to fill herself. Peter caught her hips to hold her still with one arm while his other hand unbuttoned her. Fortunately the sleeve ruffles were on an elastic band. Neither would have had patience to undo two more buttons. Even as he pulled the camisole off, Peter pulled her up a little so his mouth could reach her breast. Linda cried out, clutching his head to her, squirming against him until he had to move with her and his shaft slid inside her.

Linda plunged down; Peter's lips tightened on her nipple, then loosened a little so he could gasp when she rose. The sucking sensation drove her wild and her frantic movements rocked him back. Peter had to let go of her hips with one hand to support himself, only his arm trembled so violently that Linda could feel him shake. She should have known that was a sign of imminent collapse, but for once everything was drowned by the need that was driving her.

Suddenly Peter heaved, the arm around her hips tightening like a steel band as he pulled her with him. For a moment the interruption froze her, but then Peter's hands lifted her hips and pulled them down as he moved under her. Linda cried out with relief, first catching his rhythm and then urging him faster. She rocked and squirmed, hearing Peter moaning under her, feeling his muscles tense as he fought against his imminent climax.

Finally Peter drew so hard on her breast that he hurt her. Usually Linda hated to be hurt while making love, but this time the sensation seemed to explode all through her body. She shrieked and shrieked again, then realized where she was and bit back the rest of her cries, burying her mouth in her lover's hair until she came to rest.

That was only for a moment, however. Peter was heaving against her, his head thrown back, his mouth open, sucking air. Linda began to move in time with his thrusts, bending her head to kiss his throat and stretching a hand behind her to scratch gently at his testicles. She could feel the muscles working in his neck and clamped her mouth on his just in time to muffle a howl of release. She rode him a moment more, until his hand clamped her tight against him and he pulled his lips free.

"Stop. There's no more in me."

Linda quieted, aware now that they were lying the right way on the bed. Peter must have turned them around somehow. He was a lot stronger than he looked. She smiled into his shoulder, in no hurry to separate their bodies, enjoying the pleasant contrast of the rather chilly night air on her back and the warmth of Peter under her. She only realized that Peter was not as quietly content as she when he cleared his throat awkwardly.

Before he could make some stupid conventional remark that would embarrass them both, Linda said, "Ah! Just like Maxwell House Coffee."

"What?"

"Good to the last drop."

There was a brief, awed silence; then Peter began to guffaw. Somehow, they got untangled and covered, side by side in the narrow bed with Linda's head on Peter's shoulder.

"I haven't laughed so much since before Mom died," he said softly into her hair. "I love you." She knew from the sound that he was smiling. "And you're quite right. I *was* going to say that sex hadn't changed anything. That I still wanted to marry you. How did you know I was going to say something stupid?"

Linda pulled her head away just enough so she could see him without getting cross-eyed. Peter met her eyes, and to Linda's intense surprise, his were full of tears.

Before she could speak, he went on, "It doesn't matter how. You did know. The trouble is, it's true. I want to marry you more than ever. Linda, I can't wait. I really can't. Not because I want to be in bed with you—oh, I do, but that could be managed. There are always hotel rooms and we could sneak away to sheltered coves on the beach at Corfu—I know plenty of them—but I'll tell you right now, I won't do it. I don't want to make love to you on a beach—horrible experience that is anyway. I want to marry you and live with you, see you at breakfast every day for the rest of my life, with your hair in curlers and cream all over your face."

"I don't put curlers in my hair at night, and I wash my face before I come to breakfast," Linda said.

The silly statement was all she could get out. Having been about to burst into an indignant protest against Peter's calm assumption that she would go on sleeping with him whenever he wanted, with or without marriage, she found herself with nothing to say—completely deflated by his final sentences.

"Don't split hairs. You know my aunt is a different generation from us. She doesn't think the way we do. If you leave her and marry me, she'll—she'll have a fit. She'll think it unsuitable and be bitterly angry with both of us. I can't bear for her to be hurt and angry, to feel that she'd been used and deceived. What are we going to do?"

"Avoid each other like the plague." Linda put a hand up to cover Peter's mouth and still his angry protest. Then she shook her head warningly. "Otherwise, if you're going to look at me all the time the way you're looking at me right now, your aunt is going to know what you're thinking in two minutes. She's very clever, you know."

Peter grinned. "She knows *that* already. You're the only one that didn't notice right away. That first Sunday we had dinner together, Rose-Anne told me to stop undressing you in public. That's what we argued about. But Rose-Anne has a dirty mind. To her, my intentions had to be dishonorable because you were an employee. Aunt Em just warned me that she wouldn't stand for any hanky-panky. She said you were a nice girl and I wasn't to shock you."

They both giggled over that, but Linda's laughter cut off mid-chuckle. "You know," she said, "maybe you shouldn't avoid me. Maybe it's a good idea for you to look at me like a dog following a bitch in heat. Try out a gentle hint or two, too—not about me but about getting married. Meanwhile, I'll start hinting about leaving this job when we get back to England. Old people don't like shocks, but they accept new things very well when you introduce them carefully. After all, the older one gets, the more practice one has in accepting unpalatable facts of life."

Peter sat up, frowning, but after a moment he nodded. "Mmm, maybe. You mean once she gets used to those ideas, we can start hinting about combining them."

"Yes, and if she really is as fond of me as you think, we can hold out my still being around and spending a few hours a day with her as a consolation prize. Except for arranging this trip, a companion wouldn't really have enough to do. I could take care of all her needs in a couple of hours, drive her anywhere she wanted to go, answer her mail, everything I have been doing, so she really won't miss me at all. But you can't be impatient, Peter. We have to go slowly. These weeks in Corfu, we'll have to be careful."

He didn't answer that at once but sat staring down at her, now with a mulish expression around his mouth. "Just how far does careful go?" he asked at last.

"All the way," Linda replied firmly. "I don't think I'd enjoy having you sneak into my room at night. I just couldn't concentrate on—on the kind of pleasure you've given me tonight if I had to keep one ear cocked for who was coming down the hall."

Peter shuddered. "If you yell like you did every time we make love, they'd all be coming down the hall to see who was murdering you."

"I've never made a noise like that before in my life!" Linda exclaimed indignantly. "It's your fault. And you weren't actually a mummy yourself."

"I never made a noise like that either," he said, flushing and laughing. "All right, all the way it is, but don't expect me to be cheerful or good humored about it." Then he sighed. "I'd better go. It's three o'clock."

Linda started to sit up and then realized there wasn't room for someone as uncoordinated as Peter to dress with her standing, and lay back again. "I wish you could stay," she said. "But if you don't go, I'm afraid we wouldn't get any sleep at all. And I have to get up early. After all, I'm a working girl, and your aunt went to bed right after dinner."

Peter froze, tight-lipped, and then bent over her; for a moment Linda was almost frightened by his expression, but he only dropped a kiss on the top of her head, straightened, and started to dress. From the door he smiled at her ruefully, shook his head, and went out quickly.

Linda did not sleep well despite her exhaustion. Twice she woke, shuddering, having dreamt of Peter dead of drowning. The last remnants of the horror that had touched her were at last dissipated by the bright sunlight and crisp breeze when she came out the next morning. A glance around the deck reassured her that Peter had been right about the rail. It was too high to fall over, even if one were given a hearty shove. Actually, it was odd that Peter had fallen at all, Linda thought, and then giggled. It wasn't really odd. Without the help of a shove, Peter could easily manage to trip over his own feet when standing still; perhaps no one else could, but Peter could.

The giggle caught in Linda's throat. His whole family knew that. Maybe whoever pushed him thought he would go over because he was so clumsy. And the intention was vicious, no matter how inept the attack.

Loyally, Peter had given no hint of his attacker. He seemed to assume, as had Mrs. Bates, that Linda would not be able to hide her knowledge. Linda sighed as she turned away from the rail. That was probably true, she thought, as she entered the passage to take the elevator to Mrs. Bates's suite. But Peter tended to show his emotions too. Maybe when they all gathered for breakfast, she would get some hint from his manner.

Special arrangements had been made so that, even though not every member of the party was traveling first class, they could all eat together. Linda found Mrs. Bates in a very sprightly mood. She wanted to hear all about the dance, and Linda gave her a humorous description of her evening's activities—except, of course, the attack on Peter and what had happened afterward in her cabin. By the time she finished, they had reached the dining room, where the remainder of their party was waiting.

"It's wonderful what being on shipboard will teach you about people," Linda remarked as they sat down.

Rose-Anne looked up sharply from the menu she had picked up. "What's that supposed to mean?" she asked.

Peter looked up too, his face a courteous blank. Don't overdo it, Linda thought. Everyone already knows you like me.

"I learned that Donald has perfect balance," she said innocently. "And that's as rare a quality as perfect pitch, you know. He never lost a single step when the ship moved—and he was the only man I danced with who didn't."

"Thank you, ma'am," Donald bowed his head in formal recognition of the compliment.

Mrs. Bates laughed. "I've been hearing all about last night's dissipations."

"Oh, have you? And did you hear that Linda is an accomplished cradle snatcher?" The remark might have been thoroughly unpleasant, but Rose-Anne's voice was light and teasing.

"Alas, too true," Linda confessed, pretending to hide her face in shame. "My most devoted attendant swain was about sixteen or seventeen—" Her voice checked and her eyes widened in horror. "And I have the horrible feeling that my evil deed is going to haunt me for the rest of this trip," she added in a murmur as the young man who had followed her out the night before made his way toward the table.

When he arrived, he asked respectfully whether Linda would play paddle tennis with him after breakfast.

"I would love to, of course," Linda replied kindly and most untruthfully, "but I'm not free. I am employed by Mrs. Bates as her companion, and my time belongs to her."

Mrs. Bates looked up. Her face was quite sober, but her eyes were dancing with mischief. "Oh, Linda, you make me out an ogre. Of course you may play paddle tennis with Mr.—er—"

"Samson," the pale, thin youth supplied.

"Yes, with Mr. Samson," Mrs. Bates concluded.

Her voice did not even quiver, although it was a trace fainter than usual, but a choking gurgle came from one of the twins. Linda bit the inside of her lip painfully, and was able to reply with composure, "Thank you very much, Mrs. Bates. And thank you for asking me, Mr. Samson. I will meet you at the courts later, at about ten-thirty."

To the intense relief of the entire party, the young man took the hint and went off. A dead silence reigned until the door of the breakfast saloon closed behind him. Then the laughter all had been choking back burst out. The general was the first to recover.

"Rolled up," he chortled, wiping his eyes. "Linda, you were rolled up—horse, foot, and guns. That will teach you to try to use Emmeline as an excuse for what you don't want to do."

Linda glared across the table at Rose-Anne and Donald. "I don't know which of you made that noise, but when I find out—you'll suffer for it. I had to take a big bite out of my lip to keep from laughing."

"You mean," Mrs. Bates interposed gently, "that you did *not* wish to play tennis with—er, Mr. Samson, Linda dear?"

"Oh, Emmeline," Mrs. Sotheby said, her voice shaking with suppressed giggles, "that was cruel. Why didn't you let Linda back out gracefully?"

Now Mrs. Bates laughed softly. "Because it wouldn't have done her the slightest bit of good. He would have gone right on asking and pursuing her. She must make it plain—whatever reason she gives—that she does not want his attentions."

"But she won't do that," Peter said, speaking for the first time. "I learned something on shipboard too, that Linda is equally kind and good-natured from her head right down to her toes. I know about the toes for sure. I stepped on them often enough last night, and she went right on dancing with me."

He smiled blandly around at the whole party and Linda had the sinking feeling that she had badly underestimated Peter's ability to conceal his thoughts—or overestimated her ability to read them. The feeling proved all too accurate. Not by the blink of an eye or the faintest inflection or hesitation of speech did he betray any difference in feeling toward any member of the party—not even toward her. She did not know whether she was more relieved that he would not betray that they were lovers or more disappointed that all hope was lost for pinpointing the deadly jester and being able to watch for and circumvent his or her moves.

As she settled Mrs. Bates into a deck chair with a book and some embroidery, and with Gertrude just behind her to run her errands if she wanted something, Linda worried away at last night's incident—not the lovemaking but the attack on Peter. Indeed, it was because a future attack might deprive her of her lover that the less attractive event and the conversation she had had about it with Peter filled her thoughts. Somewhere she had detected a false note. She had almost reached the paddle-tennis court when the inconsistency leapt out at her in plain terms. To gain time to think, she reversed direction and began to walk slowly all the way around the ship.

Linda brushed the vagueness off her idea and put it in plain terms. Whatever else Peter was, he was sane. No sane man will contemplate a lifetime of dodging attempts to murder him—no matter how fond he is of the murderer. Therefore, the danger was a short-term thing; that is, he would only need to be careful for a short time. After that, presumably, the reason for the attacks would be gone and they would stop. One attack on me, Linda thought, and one attack on Peter. The only short-term thing she

and Peter had in common—to put it crudely—
was Mrs. Bates's life.

It made good sense. The attack on her, Linda
was sure, had merely been meant to frighten.
Possibly, whoever it was had wished to remove
a watchdog while they remained in London. It
was Linda who drove Mrs. Bates and accompanied her on visits and shopping expeditions.
Doubtless, if she went alone, Mrs. Bates would
be more vulnerable to an "accident." Perhaps
the attempt to frighten Linda away was simply
because Mrs. Bates seemed fond of her; the
attacker wished to be sure Linda wouldn't creep
into the old woman's will. The attack on Peter,
inept as it was, was entirely different. It was
intended to be deadly. Because Peter already
was the beneficiary of Mrs. Bates's will?

The tennis courts loomed up again, so close
this time that Linda's waiting swain had seen
her and started forward. She had time only to
decide firmly that she would tell the general
about what had happened and her conclusions,
as soon as she could find him alone, in spite of
Peter's desire for secrecy. The general would
be able to keep an eye on Peter when Linda
could not.

Not until after dinner was Linda able to catch
General Barthemeles alone—and then she had
to run after him, catching him just as he entered
his cabin. Although he smiled as kindly as usual, he was obviously not too enthusiastic about
listening to Linda's tale. When she began, he
looked surreptitiously at his watch. By the time

she finished, however, he was chewing uncomfortably on his moustache.

"I'm sorry to hear this, very sorry," he muttered. "And, of course I'll keep an eye on Peter. But it isn't necessary, m'dear, not necessary at all. Peter's right. No danger. No real danger."

"Then why do you look so worried?" Linda asked reasonably. "And don't tell me this attack on Peter was a joke."

"No—no, it wasn't. And that answers your other question too. I'm worried because . . ." He sighed. "Whatever hard feelings there've been in this family, I never believed—" He hesitated as if he had been about to say a name, then changed his mind. "I never believed that anyone was disturbed enough to become violent."

"But you *are* worried."

"More distressed than worried, m'dear."

He looked it, and for a frustrated moment Linda was silent, but then she burst out with what she had hoped not to need to say. "All right, say Peter can take care of himself, but don't you see that the main target must be Mrs. Bates?"

The general chewed his moustache some more, but this time he wouldn't meet Linda's eyes. "Peter is the first target," he mumbled unhappily at last. "I'm sure Emmeline will be safe as long as Peter is safe." Suddenly he glanced at his watch again, this time openly. "I'm sorry I can't offer you better comfort than this, but I will watch over Peter as best as I can—though I don't think it's necessary. And

I'll talk to him again. But I *can't* do more than that, m'dear. I really can't."

Realizing that she could get no more out of the old man and that she was delaying him, although he was too polite to tell her outright to go, Linda thanked him and left. In one way she was more at ease. Partly that was because what the general said made good sense. It was unreasonable to harm Mrs. Bates while Peter was still around and still her favorite. In addition to that, General Barthemeles's clear conviction that Peter either was in no danger or could take care of anything that threatened him gave her more confidence than Peter's own assertion that he would be safe.

Nonetheless, it was quite clear to Linda that the general now knew something he had not known when she spoke to him about the attacks in London and that he had no intention of telling her what he knew. It was frustrating that all three of them—Peter, Mrs. Bates, and the General—knew who was guilty and she, who had been present at every incident, could not guess. It was frustrating, but not really strange. They all knew each other so well. Probably some characteristic act or piece of family history had identified the person.

Linda had gone out on the deck after talking to the general; she leaned on the rail and carefully rethought each attack, including, for the sake of completeness, the incident on the landing of the stairs in London. There was nothing—except the two pushes, on Mrs. Bates and on Peter—that the incidents had in common. Well, yes, there was. No weapon had been used, unless the drug in the candy could be considered a weapon. But Linda didn't see anything that could be characteristic of a person.

"All alone and palely loitering?"

Donald's voice was so soft that Linda turned her head to smile without any sense of shock. "Loitering, but not palely, I hope."

"It's the moonlight, I suppose. You do look a trifle pensive though."

Linda smiled again. "That's the moonlight and the stars. They bring out the contemplative aspect of my soul."

"And what were you contemplating?"

"Your family mostly," Linda replied, quite truthfully but with every intention to decieve.

"Why? I think we're pretty ordinary."

For a moment, Linda was stunned into silence. Two slightly homicidal attempts were ordinary? But Donald didn't—or, at least, shouldn't—know anything about those. And if he didn't—or was pretending he didn't—of course his reply was perfectly reasonable.

"It was really me with respect to the family," Linda said, ungrammatically, more for the need to give him some answer than because she was thinking of what she said.

"Oh-oh." Donald sighed. "Has Rose-Anne been at it again?"

"No—at least if you mean has she been teasing me. In fact, that's what I was thinking. From everything I've heard or read about being a companion, one is usually treated like dirt, but everyone has been kinder than kind to me."

Donald laughed. "It might have something to do with you, you know. You don't whine or snivel or sneak around sighing and sorry for yourself. But it's Aunt Em, too. She's the dearest person. Oh, maybe she's got a little crotchety since she was so sick, and she's always been a terrible tease—pulls my mother's leg all the time, and Mum has quite a temper under the flutter—but she's kind and generous in the right way. Oh, like with you and that Samson fellow. She was teasing you, but she was quite right about how to get rid of him."

"She was quite right to point out that I couldn't have it both ways. It's very sobering to realize one has prided oneself on being kind, but only wants to be kind at one's own convenience. Either kindness must be carried right through or it's just another form of cruelty."

"Oh, you caught that, did you? Didn't know our family type of innuendo would get through to you, but you're as keen as mustard—that's my mother's vintage slang. Oh, damn! You can't help loving them, but their ideas are set in concrete. Old people are the devil. They can mess up your life."

Linda was somewhat startled by the sudden intensity that broke through Donald's veneer of sophistication. She was undecided whether to put him off with some silly platitude or ask sincerely what was troubling him. In the moment that she hesitated, however, she became aware of an odd sensation. Someone was watching them. Whether some sound or a flicker of light had alerted her, she didn't know, but she was sure they were no longer alone on that portion of the deck.

Deliberately, Linda turned and looked. She saw no one and hadn't expected to see anyone. This time the chairs had been stacked. Four or five people could have been concealed in the shadows beside the stacks. As long as a person stood still, no one could see him or her without walking right over. Donald did not turn his head, Linda noted with surprise, and felt a quiver of suspicion. That was unnatural. It was quite instinctive to look when someone else did.

"I thought I heard a sound," Linda said slowly. "I think someone is watching us."

Even as she spoke, Linda realized that Donald was as aware of the intruder as she was. The very stubbornness with which he stared out to sea and the tenseness of his stance betrayed him.

"There's no one there," he said.

Quite suddenly, he moved close to her and grasped her around the waist. Linda went ice-cold, but Donald only swung her around forcibly and said, "Come on, let's get out of here and get a drink."

Chapter Thirteen

Linda's fear dissipated as suddenly as it had come upon her. Far from trying to throw her overboard, although he retained a powerful grip on her, Donald steered her promptly into the well-lit and well-populated American Bar.

"Sorry to be so forceful," he said. "The dark didn't suit my mood—or suited it too well. And I didn't feel like being alone. What will you have?"

"A Brandy Alexander," Linda replied. She allowed herself to be led to a small table near the wall and subsided into a seat meekly. By the time Donald returned with the drinks, she had decided that Mrs. Bates's lesson would be put to good use. She liked Donald and, if he wanted to talk something out, she had to listen, even if she really wanted to think about something quite different. Besides, she wasn't sure it was something different. There *had* been someone watching. Her or Donald? Was it his turn to have a nasty trick played on him?

"Anyone you're fond of can play the devil with your life," Linda remarked as he set the glasses down. His expression was petulant and faintly hostile, as it had been when she first met him. "You have to decide when it's really the devil and when it's only a little imp."

"You sound just like Rose-Anne," he said, almost in a snarl. "Just decide what you want to do, Donald, and do it. Once it's irrevocable, it will soon become acceptable," he mimicked in his sister's lanquid drawl. "Oh, yes, it will be accepted, but I know what it feels like. Rose-Anne is always doing, and I'm always accepting."

"Perhaps—" Linda had begun, when the "devil" spoken of appeared.

"Glad I tracked you down," Rose-Anne said. "Mum says Mrs. Bates wants you, Linda."

Linda looked up, surprised. "I thought she was settled for the evening playing bridge. Well, duty calls, I—"

"You can finish your drink." Rose-Anne settled into a chair at the table. "When Aunt Em is playing bridge, she never notices the time. Besides, how's she to know how long it took me to find you?"

Linda had had every intention of finishing her drink before going, but Rose-Anne's remark—

implying that it would be taking a sneaking advantage to linger because Mrs. Bates couldn't know—annoyed her. She got up at once.

"Sorry about the drink, Donald, but beggars can't be choosers."

"Oh, Linda, I say, a minute or two—"

Had he scoffed at Rose-Anne's remarks, Linda would have remained, but he said nothing to his sister. "I wouldn't want to cheat on my employer's time, especially when she wouldn't know." Linda turned her head to look contemptuously at Rose-Anne, who was at a slight disadvantage sitting down. "Or would she?" Linda finished in a sarcastic drawl.

She had the satisfaction of seeing Rose-Anne flush. Whether the emotion was due to rage or shame, Linda had no idea and didn't care. It was satisfaction enough to have gotten a rise out of the cool woman. In fact, she wasn't nearly as annoyed with Rose-Anne as she might have been because the interruption had saved her from Donald's confidences.

Mrs. Bates was playing with the total absorption she gave to bridge, and Linda waited quietly until the hand was finished. "Did you want me, Mrs. Bates?" she asked while the next hand was being dealt out.

"Goodness, where did you appear from so fast? I hope my message didn't interrupt anything important." Her eyes narrowed. "I only said you should stop by when you were free."

"I wasn't doing anything important." But Linda's nod and grin confirmed Mrs. Bates's suspicions. "I was only having a casual drink with Donald. What can I do for you?"

"That Rose-Anne." Mrs. Bates sighed. "Oh, well, since you are here . . . Will you run up and tell Gertrude not to wait up for me?" The old lady smiled impishly. "I have finally found some satisfactory partners and, since I don't feel at all tired, I intend to play for a while."

Linda nodded and was about to ask whether she should come back, but the cards had been dealt and Mrs. Bates reached for her hand. To distract a bridge player, Linda knew, was almost as heinous as making noise on a golf course before a crucial putt, so she withdrew softly.

A tap on Mrs. Bates's door got no response. Linda knocked a little louder, but still received no reply. Her first guess was that Gertrude had gone out, but just as she turned away she had second thoughts. It wasn't like Gertrude to leave without letting Mrs. Bates know. Linda thought the maid might be in the bathroom, and she tried the door. It swung open at once. That was a sure sign that Gertrude was somewhere in the suite. She would never leave the door unlocked.

The sitting room was empty. Linda went to the tiny writing desk to sit down and wait a few moments. She knew well enough that nothing was more annoying than being interrupted while in the bathroom, and she had no intention of sitting on the soft chairs and creasing the cushions that Gertrude no doubt had fluffed and smoothed to perfection. A thin sheaf of papers, carbon copies of business letters with Peter's name at the bottom, was lying there. Linda stood up hastily. Prying into Mrs. Bates's affairs would be worse than creasing cushions, and she knew her eyes would be drawn to the letters if she stayed where she was.

When Linda moved, the chair squeaked faintly, and it occurred to her that it was very quiet in the suite. If Gertrude was in the bathroom, there should be some sounds. Linda tapped softly on Gertrude's bedroom door. No response. She opened the door and peeped in. The room was dark, which immediately implied that Gertrude was not likely to be in the bathroom. One doesn't turn off the lights in the bedroom when taking a shower. The idea was promptly confirmed when Linda realized that the angled panel lit by the shaft of light from the sitting room was the open lavatory door. For a moment Linda felt alarmed again, wondering where Gertrude could be, but then a soft snore made her laugh silently at herself. Of course, Gertrude was in bed and asleep.

I'm getting suspicious of everything, Linda thought sheepishly. Nonetheless, she opened the door a little wider until the light fell across the bed. It was Gertrude, sound asleep. Linda closed the door hastily, afraid the light would disturb the sleeping woman and backed out, feeling much relieved. At the suite's outer door, however, she paused. Would Gertrude go to bed and leave the door unlooked?

That might have been an accident, Linda thought, as she locked the door behind her. Nonetheless, she returned to the card room and was pleased to find Mrs. Bates the dummy and free to talk.

"Gertrude was already asleep," Linda said, "but—"

Mrs. Bates tsked. "Poor woman. I saw she was tired. I should have told her to go to bed when I left. I hope she will not have a stiff neck from falling asleep in a chair."

"But she wasn't in a chair, Mrs. Bates. She was in bed, and the door was open—unlocked, I mean."

Mrs. Bates made no reply, but her face was suddenly tense and, to Linda, she looked frightened. "That isn't like Gertrude at all," she said, a little breathlessly. Then her expression cleared. "Oh, Peter must have seen she was tired and told her to go to bed. I met him in the corridor—he was bringing me some papers, but I was late and didn't want to stop so I told him to leave them in the room."

"He did. I saw some papers on the writing desk. But isn't it odd for Gertrude to leave the door unlocked if she was going to bed? Do you have the key?"

"The key?" Mrs. Bates's echo of the words was tremulous, and Linda thought she looked frightened again, but so fleetingly that she couldn't be sure, and then Mrs. Bates uttered an uncertain little laugh. "How silly of me, no, I don't have it. Oh, dear, if you locked the door, as I suppose you did, I'll have to wake poor Gertrude to get in."

"No," Linda said. "I can get a pass key from the steward or the purser. That's no problem. But Mrs. Bates, Gertrude would never tell Peter to lock the door and go to bed if she knew you had no key. She just wouldn't."

"No, of course she wouldn't." But Mrs. Bates seemed to have recovered her self-possession. She smiled and shook her head. "What Gertrude did, I am sure, is to give Peter the key and tell him to bring it to me. He'll have forgotten—and it's no good asking him because he'll deny it. Peter is a dear boy, but he does get so stubborn. He will not admit mistakes."

Linda looked and felt perfectly blank. she knew Peter pretty well—a lot better than Mrs. Bates guessed, no doubt, and he was stubborn sometimes, but not that way. When he forgot something, he was more inclined to laugh and cry *mea culpa*, as busy people do, than to lie about it. Linda almost said it aloud, but Mrs. Bates, who had been keeping one eye on the card table, interrupted her.

"I must go back, dear, the hand is finished. Go along now and enjoy yourself."

"I think I'll wait until you're through and go up with you, Mrs. Bates. It isn't right for you to run around looking for the steward."

Mrs. Bates cast her eyes heavenward and laughed. "Another protector! Linda, I may be an old lady, but I can ring the corridor bell for the steward myself. Don't you dare sit here and wait. I'll feel your impatient presence every minute and mess up every hand. Run along now."

"But this is my job," Linda protested. "You'll make me feel guilty about accepting my salary—and I need it."

"Very well." Mrs. Bates smiled ruefully. "You may come back"—she glanced at her watch—"at eleven-thirty. We won't be done before then, and by then I may want an excuse to leave if the others plan to continue playing."

Linda had barely left the card room when she ran into Peter, who had been looking for her.

"Where've you been?" he asked. "Donald said you were with my aunt, but I looked in a few minutes ago and you weren't."

"Mrs. Bates sent me to tell Gertrude not to wait up for her. Peter, did you see Gertrude when you dropped off those papers?"

"Sure. Why? Was she gone?"

"No, she's in bed, asleep, but the door to the suite was open."

"In bed? That's odd. She was yawning her head off when I went in, and I said she should go to bed, but she said Aunt Em had gone out without the key so she had to wait up for her. We had a drink together. I thought either it would wake her up or she would fall asleep on the couch. She'd hear, though, if Aunt Em knocked. But the door—" Peter stopped suddenly and his lips folded tight together. After a moment, he asked, "She was all right, wasn't she?"

"Well, her breathing sounded normal. I didn't go in because I didn't want to wake her up.

Besides, I never thought there was anything wrong."

"You locked the door?"

"Yes, of course."

"Good. Then Gertrude will be fine. And we can come back and see Aunt Em safely to her suite. Then we'll be sure she's safe and sound, too. Now you can forget about it. What shall we do? Have a drink? See the movie?"

Linda simply glared at him. Finally she gained sufficient control of her voice not to scream. "Just forget the whole thing and everything will be fine, eh?" she remarked gently. "Fine and dandy. Oh, yeah! Do you know that someone was watching and listening when Donald met me on the deck this evening?"

"You didn't say anything to me about intending to meet Donald."

"Don't be a fool, Peter. We met by accident. The important thing is that someone was hiding in the shadows by the chairs, spying on us. Should we warn Donald?"

"Hmm? You're beautiful. Let's take a walk around the deck."

"Peter! Is Donald in danger? Should we warn him?"

"No. I'll swear by anything you like that Donald is in no danger at all. Linda, please stop worrying at this business. It's annoying and perhaps even frightening for you, but I'm sure no one is in real danger. Darling, it's important that you try to put it out of your mind and act naturally. Please try."

He was serious. Linda couldn't doubt that. She wavered mentally for a moment or two, then made her decision. Either she loved and trusted Peter and believed him or here and now she had to tell him they were finished because she didn't trust and believe him. With a soft sigh Linda slipped her arm through his.

"Okay. I'll try—for a little while. But, Peter, I'm not that kind of person. And I guess you should know that I won't be that kind of wife. I don't like to walk blind, and I'm used to making my own decisions, not being told what's good for me."

"It isn't that, Linda. If it was something to do with me, I'd tell you."

"I believe that, which is why I said I'd try. You know your family and I don't—not yet. But when I do know them, don't think I'll be this docile."

Peter didn't reply at once and Linda could see the struggle taking place in him. Quite plainly he wished to unburden himself of the whole story, but he was afraid to do so. Had Linda been able to guess what was holding him back, she would have tried to resolve his doubts. She thought it likely that he felt identifying the vicious prankster would establish strains in Linda's future relations with his family.

Unfortunately, Linda could not assure him he was wrong. She didn't believe she would be capable of warmth toward anyone who had tried—no matter how ineptly—to kill Peter. In fact, she knew she could never agree that such a person was harmless. Anyone who could attempt murder for one reason had a sick enough mind eventually to commit murder for that reason or for some other reason, when the circumstances were right.

Chapter Fourteen

Mrs. Bates looked up when Peter and Linda approached her at the end of a rubber a little after eleven-thirty. "Ah, here come my wardens," she said with a smile. "I'm afraid my period of freedom is at an end."

Her table companions laughed, and the scorer began to tot up the points. Everyone seemed delighted with the game and Mrs. Bates's partner asked eagerly whether she would play again the following evening. She said she couldn't because they were to disembark at Corfu and added that she was sorry they had found each other so late. The score was remarkably even, but Mrs. Bates had the additional treat of winning a few shillings. She was, therefore, in high good humor while Peter and Linda escorted her to her suite. The steward was already waiting to open the door, having been alerted by Linda ahead of time.

Since Gertrude was asleep, Linda offered to help Mrs. Bates prepare for bed but was refused with laughter. Nonetheless, Peter insisted on glancing around the suite and that Mrs. Bates step into Gertrude's room and check on her. For a moment Linda thought Mrs. Bates was going to lose her temper, but she only sighed, laughed, and trotted softly into the maid's room.

"She's fine, sleeping rather heavily, but she must be tired with all this traveling. Gertrude isn't as young as she once was, you know."

"All right, Aunt Em," Peter replied, "but if she doesn't wake at her usual time in the morning, you call the ship's doctor right away, you hear?"

"I am not deaf," Mrs. Bates snapped, "and I assure you that if I had the faintest suspicion that anything was wrong with Gertrude, I wouldn't wait until morning to call the doctor. I happen not only to be fond of Gertrude but dependent on her—and I am not a fool."

"Oh, Peter," Linda said when they were out in the corridor again, "Why did you say that? She's so fond of Gertrude. Surely she wouldn't take any chances without you telling her."

Oddly, Peter didn't turn his head to look at her. Eyes straight ahead, he said, "I suppose you're right. All I did was annoy her. But Aunt Em has been funny about doctors since she was ill."

The rest of the evening was pleasant enough to drive the problem right out of Linda's head, but it recurred with renewed intensity when she paid her customary morning visit to determine Mrs. Bates's plans for the day. Gertrude opened the door promptly enough, but her eyes were heavy-lidded and dull.

"Gertrude," Linda exclaimed, "you look awful. Do you feel all right?"

"To tell the truth, Miss, I don't. I nearly couldn't wake up this morning, and my head is that heavy and achy, I don't know what's the matter."

"Do you have a fever?"

"No, I don't. And I felt just fine yesterday. I don't feel *sick*, Miss Linda, just dopey."

Dopey was the key word. Linda's breath drew in sharply. The symptoms, now that she was alerted to them, were all too familiar. Plenty of Linda's friends had found their sleep in a bottle of pills. Gertrude had been drugged.

"Have you seen Mrs. Bates this morning?" Linda asked quickly.

"Yes." Gertrude lowered her voice. "She seems a little annoyed about something. Maybe you better go in right away. I shouldn't have kept you here talking."

As long as the older woman was safe, Linda didn't mind if she was cross. She tapped at the door and was told in a rather brisk voice to come in.

"Good morning, Mrs. Bates."

"Good morning. Now, Linda, you are a dear girl to be so concerned over Gertrude and myself, but you should realize that elderly

213

people do not sleep as well as young ones."

"But I do realize it, Mrs. Bates. Did I come too early this morning and wake you?"

"You don't consider two A.M. too early?"

"Two o'clock!" Linda exclaimed, and stopped abruptly, recalling that Peter had left her cabin just before two, although she had wanted him to stay. He had said, sourly, that Donald had already made pointed remarks about his late return the night before that. Then she went on smoothly, "I must have been fast asleep at two o'clock in the morning. And even if I hadn't been, I would scarcely come calling at such an hour."

Mrs. Bates stared silently at Linda for a few seconds and then asked, almost pleadingly, "You mean you didn't come and try my door at two o'clock?"

"No, of course I didn't. Why in the world should I? Peter looked the door when we left you last night."

"Are you sure?" Mrs. Bates asked quickly.

"Yes, he pushed the button. I saw him do it."

Mrs. Bates shook her head. "That lock must be faulty. You know, I was a little cross when you left last night—I think I was a bit overtired. Too much bridge." Mrs. Bates smiled guiltily and a little apologetically. "I didn't notice Peter setting the lock, so I checked it. It must have sprung open. Will you tell the purser that there is something wrong with it?"

"Yes, I will," Linda replied slowly. "Is there

anything else you want done before breakfast?"

"No, nothing. And I'm sorry to have scolded you, Linda. I should have known you wouldn't be so silly as to come fooling with the door in the middle of the night."

"I wish it had been me. I don't like it, Mrs. Bates. Who would try to get into your suite—and why?"

"No one." Mrs. Bates laughed. "It must have been another passenger, perhaps one who was under the weather—or under the influence, as the saying is."

The suggestion was not unlikely, but Linda felt uneasy and unconvinced. She hurried through her breakfast and rushed back to Mrs. Bates's suite with the excuse that she wanted to help Gertrude pack for their disembarkation that afternooon. When the packing was complete, she accompanied Mrs. Bates out to the deck for her gentle prelunch walk, saying that Gertrude was still not feeling quite the thing and might like a nap. Mrs. Bates raised her brows and smiled quizzically, but she did not protest.

On the second lap of their walk, they met the general and Mrs. Sotheby. They finished the lap together and then settled down in deck chairs to enjoy the sea breeze and the warm sun. Somewhat later, Peter found them chatting comfortably about the house in Corfu and the old friends Mrs. Bates and Mrs. Sotheby expected to see there.

"Come and make a foursome at shuffleboard,

Linda," Peter said, then added, "It's okay if she goes, isn't it, Aunt Em?"

"Of course," Mrs. Bates replied, smiling.

"Oh, I'm so comfortable," Linda protested, "and shuffleboard really isn't my favorite sport. Besides, I'm enjoying the introduction I'm getting to the colony on Corfu. It's a big help to keep me from putting my foot in my mouth."

"Oh, dear," Mrs. Sotheby murmured. "I had almost forgotten you were here, Linda. Go along, do. This kind of gossip isn't meant for your ears."

Both the general and Mrs. Bates laughed aloud.

"Harriet, you are incredibly innocent," Mrs. Bates said. "I'm sure the type of gossip Linda and her friends exchange would burn your ears right off your head. This must be very dull for Linda, only she's too conscientious to leave me alone and Gertrude doesn't feel perfectly well this morning."

"It's all right, m'dear," General Barthemeles added. "We'll stay with Emmeline and take her in to lunch. You go ahead."

"But—"

"No buts," Peter insisted. "I need you worse than Aunt Em does. Rose-Anne won't partner me because she doesn't like losing, and there's a predatory female with large front teeth just itching to share my fate."

Mrs. Bates laughed again. "It's the helpless way you bump into things that attracts rabbit-toothed females, Peter. You should learn to be more graceful. But aunts must be indulgent. Go and save Peter from the fate he deserves, Linda. I will see you at lunch."

There was nothing Linda could do except obey her employer's instructions, but she was annoyed. So was Peter. As soon as they were out of earshot of their elders, he asked sharply, "Why are you hanging around my aunt like a leech today? Are you trying to make her nervous?"

"I don't need to make her nervous," Linda replied with equal sharpness. "Someone drugged Gertrude last night, Peter. Damn it, don't shake your head at me. She had all the symptoms of it this morning."

"Now look, Linda, you're letting your imagination run away with you. You're starting to see assassins behind every pile of chairs and poisoners in every corner. How could you know Gertrude was drugged?"

"Because I've got a hell of a lot of experience with the morning-after-a-sleeping-pill night look." Linda was so angry that she didn't notice the somewhat startled and speculative glance Peter directed at her. She went on heatedly, "I never said anyone tried to poison Gertrude. I said someone wanted her asleep—sound asleep—last night. Peter, did you lock your aunt's door when we left?"

"Of course I did. You saw me do it."

"Well, then, someone tampered with that lock, because Mrs. Bates had to relock it after we left." Linda thought she saw a brief frown, followed by tightened lips, which she interpreted as anxiety, but the expression was wiped to bland attention before she could be certain. She prodded him with, "And someone tried to get into her suite last night."

"How do you know that?" Peter's voice was sharp.

"Mrs. Bates told me," Linda snapped. "She thought I was checking on her and scolded me for waking her."

"Did Aunt Em say someone tried to get in?"

Linda blinked at the nitpicking and then, wondering whether it had a purpose she didn't understand, said, "No. After I told her I was asleep by then—which I should have been—she said it must have been a tipsy fellow passenger, but I don't believe that. She may not either. She certainly didn't object as she usually does when I offered to stay around today."

To this Peter made no reply except to shake his head. Linda thought he was angry, but they arrived at the shuffleboard courts at that moment and it was impossible for her to discover why or at whom he was annoyed. The game was a good idea. It gave Linda an opportunity to express her own bad temper in an acceptable manner, and she played so furiously that, although she and Peter did lose, it was only by one unlucky point at the very end.

They all came in to lunch in restored good humor, describing their games in strophe and antistrophe throughout the meal to a willing and indulgent audience. After the meal, Linda saw Mrs. Bates to her cabin for her after-lunch nap. Gertrude was there, looking much better, and Linda went away with a clear mind to a very busy afternoon. She had to check all the luggage, make sure nothing was left behind, and see that the stewards collected it for disembarkation later that afternoon.

General Barthemeles had already changed into his shore-going clothes. He was an efficient packer by long experience, and Linda had little to do in his cabin beyond opening drawers and the closet door to make sure nothing had rolled into a dark corner and been overlooked. She saw the steward of their corridor load her bags and the general's and moved on to the cabin shared by Peter and Donald.

This was less tidy. A bottle of mouthwash and a packet of asprins were still in the medicine cabinet. Linda dropped them into the tote she carried for collection of leftover items. A dark maroon sweater was lying on the floor of the closet. That went into the tote bag too. There was nothing in the drawers. Linda didn't turn for a knock on the door but called, "Come in," imagining it was the steward to collect the valises.

"Mr. Peter?"

Linda turned sharply. "Gertrude? Peter isn't here. Is something wrong? Is Mrs. Bates all right?"

"Why, yes. Madam was lying down for her rest and I got a call saying that Mr. Peter wanted to speak to me. It's funny he isn't here."

"Did he say to meet him here?"

"Well, no. But he didn't say anywhere else, and where else could he mean?"

Suddenly fear and suspicion gripped Linda. "Gertrude," she said hurriedly, "you wait here for a few minutes until the steward comes. Make sure he takes all the valises—and if Peter hasn't shown up by then, you can ask if the steward has seen him. I'm going to make sure Mrs. Bates is all right."

In her hurry, Linda forgot to ask Gertrude for her key. Had the door been locked, she would have remembered as soon as she couldn't turn the knob. However, even as she came down the corridor, Linda could see that it was not even shut. Gertrude would not have left the door open no matter how briefly she expected to be away. Linda broke into a run and then stopped short, gasping with fright. Through the small aperture she could see the sole of a shoe.

The paralysis that held her did not last long. Cold as ice and wrenchingly reluctant, Linda forced herself forward. One part of her mind screamed at her to hurry, that Mrs. Bates might have fainted or had a heart attack and moments could be important, but under that, something warned that the old woman was dead—not of natural causes but horribly murdered. And as Linda's hand fell on the knob, it occurred to her that she had never seen death. She had seen the preludes, the comas and convulsions, but not death itself.

In that second frozen moment, before Linda could nerve herself to apply the pressure that would open the door and expose the truth, quick footsteps sounded. Such relief flooded her that she felt weak. Whoever it was, at least she wouldn't be alone.

"Oh, please," she began, but her voice was only a whisper and she found she could not see the approaching person clearly.

The footsteps accelerated. A strong arm slid around her waist. "Linda! What is it?"

"Peter!" This time relief gave strength. "Your aunt," she gasped, gesturing toward the door, which she had released.

Peter demonstrated the depth of his anxiety by the lack of ceremony with which he released Linda, almost thrusting her away as he opened the door. Now that she was not alone, Linda recovered her self-possession. She was right on Peter's heels as he entered the room, and she went down on her knees beside Mrs. Bates, who was lying flat on the floor.

The first thing of which Linda was conscious was that her employer was not dead. The color in her face was normal, and her breathing was light and even. Peter was already at the phone, calling the ship's doctor, and Linda took the older woman's wrist in her fingers. The pulse did not flutter or hesitate. It seemed strong and steady. Linda had little medical knowledge, but it did not seem to her that Mrs. Bates was in any immediate danger.

"Doctor's coming," Peter said, as he came to kneel by his aunt too.

"Good, but I don't think you need to worry,

Peter. Look, her color and breathing are good and her pulse is good too. It's funny she should be lying flat like this—as if someone straightened her out."

Peter didn't answer. He merely sat on his heels and stared down at Mrs. Bates with a worried frown. A moment later, this expression was replaced by a smile because Mrs. Bates's eyes opened slowly. Linda did notice that, though his lips smiled, his eyes remained worried. She also noticed that Mrs. Bates didn't look dazed or confused when her eyes opened on Peter but very frightened. Her breath caught and she turned her head almost the way a trapped animal turns away from its captor. On seeing Linda, her whole body relaxed.

"Oh, dear," she murmured plaintively, "I must have had a dizzy spell."

"Don't move, Aunt Em," Peter said. "The doctor's on his way. He'll—ah!" A knock had sounded on the door and Peter jumped to his feet. "Here he is."

The ship's doctor, thin, grey-haired, grey-moustached, entered quietly and took his stethoscope from his bag.

"Shall I carry her to the bed?" Peter asked.

"One moment," the doctor replied. He pushed Mrs. Bates's suit jacket aside and listened. Then he smiled a formal smile. "Yes, please move her to the bed."

Peter gathered up Mrs. Bates as easily and as tenderly as if she were a small child, making nothing of her plump figure. Linda had started to follow, think she might be of assistance in removing Mrs. Bates's clothing, when Gertrude ran in.

"Miss, Miss, I saw the doctor. What happened?"

"We don't know, Gertrude. When I came, the door was a little open and Mrs. Bates was lying on the floor."

"On the floor?" Gertrude whispered. "Oh, God, my God, is she very bad?" The maid's voice trembled and tears filled her eyes.

Linda took her hand. "No, I don't think so. She spoke quite naturally when she came to, and her breathing was good. She wasn't pale or gasping or clammy."

At that moment, Peter came out. "Linda, if you could—Oh, Gertrude, that's even better. Aunt Em's been asking for you. Will you go in and give the doctor a hand? Don't look so worried. He seems to think she's all right."

When Gertrude had hurried in and closed the door behind her, Linda asked Peter whether he had said that to comfort the maid or because it was true.

"You can't comfort people with lies on such a subject," he said harshly. "My aunt doesn't seem to have had another heart attack or—at least, that was all the doctor cared to say in front of her." Then his expression became gentler. "I'm sorry you had such a scare, darling. Are *you* all right?"

"Yes, of course. Just ashamed of being so weak-kneed."

Peter smiled faintly, but there didn't seem to be anything more to say and they waited silently. In about fifteen minutes the thin, grey doctor came out.

"You are her nephew? Her closest relative, she said."

Peter stiffened as if to resist a blow. "I . . . yes."

"Walk down the corridor with me. Ah, young lady—Linda, the companion?"

"Yes, I am. Is there anything I can do to help?" Linda asked eagerly.

"No." The doctor smiled. "Mrs. Bates is not ill. Whatever small seizure she may have had left no lasting effects. She will be able to leave the ship this afternoon. Let her rest until then—and *don't* ask her how she feels every five minutes. Act, if you can, as if nothing occurred."

Peter returned very soon and beckoned Linda out to him. He smiled at her, although his eyes were sad. "He just wanted to ask whether I knew of my aunt's heart condition. When I said yes, he shrugged and gave me the same advice he'd just given you. Damn it. I wish he was the doctor on Corfu instead of that quack. Well, never mind. He doesn't know what happened. Maybe a tiny—a little dizzy spell. But there's nothing they can do about that either. He said that the medication she's taking is what he would recommend himself."

Linda shook her head. "Did you ever know anyone who had a dizzy spell to fall down so neatly? People don't fall flat—not without cracking their heads open—they crumple. I think she was frightened and fainted, and then whoever frightened her straightened her out."

"But who—Oh, forget it. I don't care what happened as long as Aunt Em's all right. I— oh, Gertrude, how's my aunt feeling?"

"Fine," Gertrude said, but her face wasn't happy. Then she sighed. "She does feel all right now, I think," she added reassuringly, "but whatever happened, she seems frightened and not willing to talk about it. I never should have left her, but I was so sure she was napping and . . . What did you want, Mr. Peter?"

"What did I want? Oh, you mean when I came back here. I wanted those papers I left last night. Aunt Em said she was through with them, and—"

"No, I mean what did you want to see me about? And why couldn't you come here?"

"But I *did* come here. What do you mean, what did I want to see you about?"

"Mr. Peter, stop it. I'm upset enough. You phoned me and said you had to talk to me—"

"Phoned you? When?"

"Oh, I don't know—"

Linda looked at her watch. "It must have been about half or three-quarters of an hour ago, because that's when I saw you in Peter's cabin, Gertrude."

"I certainly didn't phone you this afternoon," Peter said indignantly. "What for? I was coming here anyway."

"Are you saying I made that call up? Or that

225

I'm lying?" Gertrude flushed with anger and shame.

"Good God, no!" Peter exclaimed. "Of course not. I'm sure someone called you. Why the hell should you tell such a stupid lie, and right to my face? All I'm saying is that *I* didn't phone."

"But Peter"—Linda's voice sounded odd to her and she swallowed—"that means that someone deliberately phoned to get Gertrude to leave the suite."

"Yes." Peter's face was now totally expressionless, and the glance he turned on Linda was forbidding.

Her lips had parted to speculate on the reason anyone should want to get Gertrude out of the way, but she didn't utter the words. When Peter wanted, he could be remarkably formidable.

Gertrude had paid little attention to this exchange. She was frowning in concentration and finally said, "I guess it wasn't you, Mr. Peter. Now I think back, the voice was funny and the words weren't the way you say them, not the way I'm used to. But you know I don't like the telephone. I'll tell you one thing sure, though. It wasn't Mr. Sotheby playing one of his tricks. He says his words like madam."

"She means," Peter said with a smile, "that Donald speaks like an English gentleman and I don't."

"That's right," Gertrude said. "Oh, I don't mean you aren't a gentleman, Mr. Peter, but your voice is foreign, deep like, and you say 'here' and 'I' different."

"All right, Gertrude." Peter grinned at her. "I didn't take any offense." Then his face grew grave. "You stay here now, no matter what happens. I *won't* call you away. If I need you, I'll come here. And if anyone else phones, just tell them you can't leave Aunt Em. We'll be off this ship and into the house soon, so there won't be any more funny business."

Linda looked at her watch once more and made an exasperated sound. "It's awfully late. I have to check the cabin Rose-Anne and Mrs. Sotheby used. Oh, Gertrude, you didn't send the tote bag with the steward, did you?"

"No, Miss. It's on one of the beds in Mr. Peter's cabin."

"Then I'll be off and get the luggage finished."

"I'll come with you," Peter offered.

"Don't you dare!" Linda cried. "I can't afford to be distracted while I'm getting you off this ship in one piece."

Chapter Fifteen

Disembarkation went smoothly and, to Linda's surprise, Mrs. Bates seemed very spry. Linda would have liked to call ahead and have the doctor meet them at the dock, but Peter protested vehemently against the idea and, when Linda hinted it to Mrs. Bates, she asked in a puzzled way why she should want to see a doctor. Linda said no more. If Mrs. Bates didn't remember what had happened, she had no intention of reminding her.

Customs were also very simple. Mrs. Bates had been wintering on Corfu for many years and was well known. Moreover, all the heavy luggage had already been inspected and sent up to the house. There was little to do beyond exchanging greetings and waiting for the luggage from the ship to be loaded into taxis. Mrs.

Bates did not even wait for that. As soon as her passport was checked and she had enquired about this officer's children and that officer's wife and mother, Gertrude shepherded her out to her automobile, which was already waiting. The general and Mrs. Sotheby went with her. Peter, Donald, and Rose-Anne shared a cab, and Linda and Gertrude waited to go up with the luggage.

Gertrude was still very distressed over Mrs. Bates's faint. Over and over she said she couldn't understand what was wrong with her mistress. "She isn't acting right," the elderly maid complained, shaking her head.

Linda said what she could to calm her, explaining that elderly people often wished to ignore signs of ill health and sometimes did behave differently after even a mild seizure. It didn't seem to Linda that she had said anything significant, but Gertrude seemed relieved. Finally, the luggage was stowed and the cab began its long climb away from the harbor.

In the area around the pier where the passenger ship had tied up, there were many shops displaying typically tourist wares. Perhaps, Linda thought, gazing at the riot of color in the Turkish section, where carpets were hung on racks and walls and piled on tables, typical was the wrong word. The brilliant chaos of colors was familiar; it reminded her of the shops that sold silk scarves in French ports. She grinned briefly as she wondered whether these "oriental" rugs were made in Dutch factories, as "French" and "Italian" silk scarves—when the label was inspected—might be products of Taiwan and Hong Kong.

The Greek shops displayed Greek pottery, possibly even made in Greece, and figured cloth, more probably milled in Japan or even the United States. Linda, having previously traveled with a group too sophisticated to visit such obvious "tourist traps," promised herself a trip back to town on her day off and some happy hours scrounging through the fascinating wares. She was beginning to think that the sneered-at tourists had a lot more fun than her worldly-wise friends.

She was delighted at the change in perspective that being a "poor working girl" had produced. The idle rich, who were supposed to be free to do as they liked, actually had most of their pleasure severely curtailed by stupid notions of what was beneath them or a fear—often far greater than that in people to whom money was a hard-won prize—of being cheated. *But I can't be cheated*, Linda thought, smiling. *I'm not making an investment. If I buy something because I like it, I've got what I paid for in the pleasure the thing gives me and the pleasure of looking for it and buying it.*

She found that her ruminations had carried her right out of the district she was thinking about. The cab, not in its first youth—Linda grinned again at that miracle of understatement—rattled and groaned over the narrow cobblestone street. The houses that fronted it reminded her somewhat of towns in southern France and Sicily. They had flat stucco faces with faded red and green shutters closed tight against the sun. The street wound upward sharply, so sharply at times that Linda thought the cab was going to give up. The driver, however, knew his vehicle. Each time the strangling motor really sounded as if it were going to die, he would shift down, grinding and clashing the gears until Linda winced and wished she could beg for mercy for them.

Nonetheless they went steadily up, soon losing sight of the sea. Soon also, the houses thinned. Here each house was surrounded by its own garden, the whitewash on the stucco faces fresh and the closed shutters bright with new paint. Only a little farther on the houses disappeared completely, except for a very small one here and there in the distance. The pavement gave way to dirt. Linda was grateful that the other two cars were well ahead, for a cloud of dust rose behind their wheels. The road was by no means smooth, but the drive took only about ten minutes longer.

At the top of another rise they turned sharply right and, surprisingly, were on pavement again. The reason was soon apparent. Doubtless this road, if not private itself, had been paid for by private contributions. One driveway and then another led off, again to the right, to quite elegant houses—some real manors, from what could be seen of them through the trees. Linda knew at once that this was an established and well-to-do foreign colony. The houses themselves, some very new and others in foreign architectural styles, told the tale. To the left of the road, gnarled olive trees stood, their grey-green foliage dry with summer drought, waiting for the winter rains. In the gardens surrounding the houses, well-watered green lawns and bright flowers replaced the fruitful but drab olive.

Farther along the paved stretch, where the houses thinned and retreated even deeper into the seclusion of their gardens and shading cypresses, Gertrude directed the driver to turn. The driveway looped, and there was the house. Linda smiled. She could have trusted Mrs. Bates's impeccable taste. Here was no transplanted English cottage or manor house. The villa was obviously native to its surroundings, a pale creamy yellow, not bright enough to dazzle the eyes in the sun but well able to reflect away heat and tinted enough to look cheerful on a grey, rainy day.

As soon as the cab pulled up, the front door opened and an elderly man, as gnarled and dry as the olives, hopped spryly out across the wide verandah. Gertrude greeted him with assurance and familiarity, and he began to unload the valises from the trunk and front seat while the driver took down what had been lashed to the roof. Linda reached for her tote and Mrs. Bates's dressing case, but the old man protested so violently that she laughed and left them to him. She was too anxious to get in and find out how Mrs. Bates had weathered the trip to spend time arguing protocol.

Linda was surprised and not too well pleased to find her employer trotting briskly around the second floor assigning rooms to everyone. Her glance at Peter was eloquent; his shrug behind his aunt's back was even more eloquent. But Linda got no chance to try her powers of persuasion. Mrs. Bates smiled at her warmly and showed her to her room, almost ordering her to look it over and then take the rest of the day to become familiar with the house, grounds, and servants.

"You know, dear," she said before Linda had a chance to get a word in, "you won't be the slightest use to me if I tell you to get my glasses from the breakfast room or the gazebo and you don't know where the breakfast room or gazebo is. And now that I have you, you can deal with the servants. You see, they don't like to take orders from Gertrude because they consider her a servant too. It is most ridiculous. Gertrude must tell me what must be done and I must tell the servants—and they aren't like English servants at all. They talk back to you and argue and tell you long personal stories." She smiled impishly. "You may have the pleasure of listening to them and getting your own way now."

"Of course, Mrs. Bates, but don't you think—"

"Not now, Linda. Whatever it is must wait. I'm too busy." She trotted away to the end of that corridor and tapped on a door. "Harriet, you don't mind being in the front of the house, do you?" she asked, sticking her head in the door. "I'm sure the road is far enough away that the noise won't . . ."

Her voice faded as she entered Mrs. Sotheby's room and shut the door behind her. Linda walked into the room Mrs. Bates had assigned to her, but at first she didn't see it at all. She now understood what was troubling Gertrude. The gushing and rushing did seem entirely unnatural for Mrs. Bates. It was puzzling. It seemed to Linda that this wasn't the type of oddity that should be produced by a minor stroke—the word Peter seemed so desperate to avoid. Dazedness, vagueness one might expect, but not all this bright efficiency. But Linda had no experience at all with the condition; what she expected came mainly from novels and an occasional article she'd read.

Linda shook her head. She'd never believe Mrs. Bates had a mild stroke on the ship. She had been deliberately frightened—in the hope that she'd have a heart attack and die?—and fainted. That's why she wouldn't talk about the experience and pretended to have forgotten it. And Mrs. Bates wasn't a silly, fluttery hostess. She had some reason for assigning people to particular rooms.

Her reasoning had come that far when Linda was interrupted by a knock on the door. Yani, the elderly factotum who had greeted them, had piled all the valises at the head of the stairs and was now distributing them. He brought in her bags with a wordless but friendly nod, then picked up the general's and brought them to the door directly across the corridor. Linda watched idly. Peter was next to Mrs. Sotheby, Rose-Anne across from her mother, and Donald opposite Peter.

As Yani trudged to and fro, Linda heard the floorboards of the corridor creak. Her first thought was that the house was old; probably it had belonged to a native resident rather than having been built in the native style for the foreign colony. Her second thought was that it was just as well she and Peter had not planned spending their nights in clandestine lovemaking. She and the general were closest to the stairs and the old man, no doubt a light sleeper, would almost certainly hear those floorboards creak if Peter wandered in the night.

Then Linda frowned. Mrs. Bates's disposition of her guests might be an accident, but Linda didn't think so. Peter was all the way at the other end of the corridor. The frown disappeared and Linda giggled softly. If Peter was right, and Mrs. Bates had noticed that he was interested in her, she had chosen a sure way to checkmate any surreptitious move Peter might plan. By the time his clumsy feet had passed down that creaking, groaning hallway, every head would be stuck out the door to see what was going on. But suddenly Linda stopped giggling.

If Mrs. Bates's intention was to stymie Peter, that was funny. But was it? Or was the arrangement the result of Mrs. Bates having been frightened on the ship? Did she want to make sure no hostile person could sneak down the stairs to her ground-floor suite? If so, wasn't it odd that the general rather than Peter was at the head of the stairs? There were two empty rooms, one on each side of the bathroom on both sides of the corridor. Then Linda nodded in recognition of Mrs. Bates's good sense. Probably the plumbing in Corfu was as noisy as that in Greece. Mrs. Bates wouldn't use the rooms next to the bathrooms unless necessary. Beside that, the elderly general would almost certainly sleep less soundly than a healthy young man who had been swimming and boating all day.

The idea stimulated in Linda a sudden desire to be out of doors. She looked quickly at her room. It was pleasant, if characterless—a double bed, a chest, a small table at which one could write, a straight chair—with two rather small windows facing more east than north. The shutters had been opened and the windows raised because the sun touched at a sufficiently oblique angle not to overheat the room. Linda leaned out. By craning forward and left, she could just make out the sea, around to the northwest.

"Hi," Donald called up. "You be careful. Those windows are awfully low. I nearly went out of one two years ago."

Linda pulled herself back with the queerest tightening of the throat and, before she realized what she was doing, glanced over her shoulder. Below, Donald laughed.

"Come down and look from here."

There was, of course, no one in the room. Linda felt foolish, remembering what Peter had said about seeing assassins in every shadow and poisoners in every corner. She *was* going all peculiar if she started taking innocent jokes as dire warnings. She leaned out again, although not as far, and called down, "All right. You can show me the gazebo. Mrs. Bates said I have to know where it is."

Of course Mrs. Bates had also told her to familiarize herself with the interior of the house and the servants, but that could wait. The bright sun, the glimpse of sparkling sea were urgent reasons to be outdoors. As it worked out, however, Linda fulfilled both orders. Donald met her at the foot of the stairs, commenting that she would never have found the back door alone.

That was probably true. The main corridor lead to a short flight of stone steps that looked as if they would open directly on the back garden. Instead the door at the bottom led into an enormous stone-floored kitchen. This room had four doors, but none of them went out to the garden and thence to the sea. One door in the back wall led to an enclosed yard that contained the vegetable garden, the shed that housed the electric generator, and the servants' cottages. The second door went to the wine cellar, the third to the scullery (which also had a door into the walled back area), and the fourth was the one they entered.

Having brought her so far, Donald introduced Linda to the staff. Aside from Yani, who still seemed to be pottering about upstairs, the inside servants were all women. Areté was Yani's wife and the cook. Persephone and Aphrodite, the upper and lower parlormaids, and Clytemnestra, the scullery maid. Linda kept her countenance and responded to the introductions gravely and properly. In fact Donald's disappointment was the only thing that made her want to smile.

"You see," she apologized on their way out, "I have been in Greece before, so I knew I was going to meet all the great mythological names attached to the most unlikely people."

"Ah, well, the best laid plans of mice and men . . ." Donald shrugged. "You could have given me my fun by looking shocked, even if you weren't—specially if you knew."

"Don't be silly," Linda replied, laughing. "I would much rather offend you than the cook or the maids. And they would have been offended because they wouldn't have understood what I was laughing or being surprised about."

Donald expressed great—and totally spurious—indignation at being considered of less importance than the cook and the maids. And, bickering in a friendly fashion, he led Linda back up the steps and sharply right, which took them directly into the dining room. Here Linda abruptly caught her breath in the middle of a sentence. Nearly the whole back wall had been removed and replaced with glass; a foreign colony addition, Linda suspected, but well worth the change in the original architecture. Spread out in a wide panorama was a curving bay—dusty green slopes, grey-black cliffs, a startling narrow band of white beach, and the sea, so blue a blue that it made the eyes ache. To the right was a formal garden, neatly broken by clean gravel paths. To the left was the most exquisite gazebo—a tiny replica of a Greek temple, its screened openings dark against the white columns.

Part of the glass wall was a sliding door, and they stepped out onto a wide verandah that surrounded three sides of the house. "Where to now?" Donald asked. "The gazebo or the sea?"

"The sea, I suppose, because—" Linda was about to say she wanted to take a look and see whether she should run back for her swimsuit, but she never got a chance to finish. Just as they stepped off the verandah, Mrs. Bates called out.

"Linda, will you come here, my dear?" And then, as Linda turned back toward the house, "No, I'm in the gazebo."

Once inside, Linda's breath was snatched away again. She had realized that the house sat up on a cliff. The views from the dining room and the verandah showed that the sea was below them, but she had expected the slope to be gentler and, certainly, she had not expected the gazebo to be perched barely a foot or so from the edge of the drop.

"My God," she breathed, "this is a kind of dangerous place to build, isn't it?"

Mrs. Bates laughed. "It wasn't so close to the edge originally. Some years ago, before my husband bought the house, there was a very bad storm—or a series of storms—that pulled out the base of the cliff and the whole thing slid down. I suppose we should have had the gazebo moved right away, but it was so beautiful—and now, who knows whether I will be back from year to year." Her voice trailed away, and she stared out over the bay.

"Don't be silly, Aunt Emmeline," Donald said. "You just like to live dangerously."

The brief melancholy was shaken off. Mrs. Bates laughed again. "It isn't really dangerous. Since we screened the gazebo in, you can't slip out and the slide gave the cliff a much broader base. Probably even a hurricane or a typhoon or whatever it is they have here couldn't damage it any more. Besides, the door on that side is kept locked." She showed Linda the latch, which was indeed larger and more secure than those usually found on a gazebo. "You see," Mrs. Bates added, "it's rusted shut. It couldn't get open by accident so, even though the door does swing out, there isn't any danger."

Linda had to agree, and she noticed that the screens were new and well fastened. It would take a more powerful push than simply falling against them to break through. Linda stood and looked out. It was a very odd sensation, like teetering at the edge of a great drop—but knowing you were perfectly safe.

"It's a lovely feeling, isn't it?" Mrs. Bates asked, coming to stand beside her. "But it really isn't nearly as high as it looks. I have never been able to decide why one gets the feeling of enormous height, almost of flying. Perhaps it's the sea below moving like that."

"Come away from there," Donald said sharply. "I know it's perfectly safe, but it gives me palpitations to watch you." He grinned apologetically as they came toward him. "Can't stand heights. They give me vertigo, and with that shifting water below this is worse than usual. I can't go near that side at all, not even at night because I know what's there."

"Oh, Donald, I'm so sorry," Mrs. Bates said remorsefully. "I forgot that. Now I remember that the first time you were here, you nearly fainted with fright when you came and looked over."

Donald looked a bit chagrined at Mrs. Bates's embarrassing memory, but Linda shook her head.

"It isn't fright," she said. "I read an article about that once. I don't remember whether its an extra delicate sense of balance or something to do with one's eyes, but height vertigo is a physical thing. It's like being tone deaf or color blind, not a disease or anything, just something you're born with. And you can't train yourself to get over it, so don't try."

"That's very interesting." Mrs. Bates smiled affectionately at Linda. "Whatever it is, I must have the opposite. I spend every minute I can out here." She sat down as she spoke in a chair facing out toward the bay. "Well, now, you children run away and play. I just wanted to show you my favorite spot, Linda."

"Can I bring you something from the house, Mrs. Bates?" Linda asked.

"No, dear. I have a bell." She showed Linda a button fixed to one of the columns not far from her seat. "It rings in the kitchen and Yani or one of the maids will come."

Having seen the bell, Linda immediately spotted the wire that ran up outside the column and discreetly across to a tree. It was quite clear that Mrs. Bates wanted to be alone, and she seemed so normal that Linda made no protest. Instead of following Donald directly to the beach, however, she said she would like a swim and must fetch her suit. Donald thought the idea an excellent one and accompanied her back to the house. On the way, Linda remarked that she had to have a word with Gertrude, and he obligingly showed her Mrs. Bates's suite off the so-called breakfast room. This was on the ground floor, a self-contained group of two bedrooms, a private sitting room, and a bath. One of the bedrooms was Mrs. Bates's. In the other Linda found Gertrude.

The maid was busy unpacking, but when Linda said that Mrs. Bates was alone in the gazebo and had not wanted company, Gertrude nodded with immediate understanding. "I'll just let this go until later," she said. "I'll go and sit out on the verandah."

"Do you want me to finish the unpacking?" Linda asked.

"No. Madam can see the beach from the gazebo. If she doesn't see you go down, she'll wonder why. She won't know I'm not unpacked, and even if she does, I'll tell her it was a long trip and I was tired. She knows I like to sit on the verandah."

Linda ran up to get her suit and down to meet Donald in the garden with a relieved mind. It was true that Gertrude might not be able to see clearly through the dark screens at that distance, but she would be able to see a shadow so that if the old woman stood up or fell out of her chair she would be aware of the movement. Besides, Linda didn't believe Mrs. Bates had been taken ill on the ship. From the verandah, Gertrude would be able to see if anyone entered the gazebo—and probably anyone who came from the house would see her sitting there.

Chapter Sixteen

The next day Linda actually worked at her job. Mrs. Bates had many friends on the island, and Linda was instructed to send them all notes to tell them her employer was back in residence. When those were dispatched, Mrs. Bates began to plan a series of small dinners and parties. Linda helped Gertrude arrange the menus and then drove the maid into the town to pick up the mail and do some shopping.

In the mail was a large separate package for Peter, who grunted irritably when he saw it and disappeared into his room, presumably to attend to the business that had followed him on vacation. It was the first intimation Linda had that Peter was not merely a glorified errand boy. Business does not follow unimportant employees. She had little time to consider the idea, however, because Mrs. Bates had by then had the time and energy to examine the garden, the cellars, and the servants' cottages. There were a stream of orders to be transmitted and a long shopping list for the next day.

Linda had snatched a few minutes for a swim in the afternoon, and Donald, who had been lounging in the garden, came down with her. At first Linda was pleased. It was much pleasanter, and safer too, to swim in company. They were having a good time, but soon Linda began to have second thoughts about spending so much time with Donald. Before the idea really came clear, Rose-Anne came down from the house. She was obviously very annoyed with Donald, but her caustic comments were evenly distributed and it was fortunate that Linda could claim, quite truthfully, that she had to get back to work.

In fact, although Linda deplored Rose-Anne's bitter and biting tongue, she was not at all sorry she had broken up the "party." Several times Donald had seemed prepared to abandon fun for some kind of serious discussion. Linda felt a little guilty about having prevented him from speaking. She knew she had to discourage any romantic ideas he had about her—if that was what had been on his mind—as soon as possible to avoid hurting him. She was not sure, however, just how to go about it. Certainly she had no intention of telling him she intended to marry

Peter—at least not until she had talked over the disclosure with Peter. And she wasn't sure how to broach the topic to Peter without arousing his quick jealousy or sounding conceited. For the moment it was easier to avoid the whole issue—but it would probably be best to avoid Donald, too, Linda thought as she walked back to the house.

That was the reason Linda left the house for a late afternoon swim almost surrepititiously the next day. She would have asked Peter to go with her, but she had not seen him at all that day. She had made an early breakfast and then gone shopping, returning to discover that Peter had gone into town in a cab to phone his office, since there was no phone in the house. Linda had exclaimed in surprise over that, but Mrs. Bates said that the service was so bad, the wires down ninety percent of the time, and the price so high, that it was not worth having an instrument installed. It was quicker, she said with twisted lips, to send one of the gardners down to the town with any message.

Linda had glanced from the dining room doors around the verandah to be sure all was clear and then examined as much as she could see of the garden from the verandah before she ventured out. She hurried across the garden, then paused at the head of the flight of stairs carved out of the cliff that led down to the beach.

The beach was empty, and Linda swung down the steps humming, her mind on the dinner party that evening. They would be putting on the dog a bit—long dresses and dinner jackets—in honor of Mrs. Paxton. It was a "thank you" party, and Linda had given considerable time and thought to the menu and the table decorations. Here, Mrs. Sotheby had unexpectedly come into her own. Linda, like most modern, city-bred women, knew nothing about flower arrangement. She had mentioned the fact to General Barthemeles.

"Yes," he agreed, smiling reminiscently, "schools don't bother with those amenities any more. My wife had a fine hand with flowers."

"Well, I don't. Do you think I should see whether there is a florist in town who will send up arrangements or a man to do them with our flowers?"

"I doubt . . . Wait, now, why don't you ask Harriet? I know she does flowers quite well. Never mind. I'll tell her to do them."

There was so much pride and possessiveness in his voice that Linda didn't protest the fact that he would be giving Mrs. Sotheby orders. In fact, his attitude strengthed Linda's notion about his relationship with Donald and Rose-Anne's mother. Somewhat later, she saw them together in the garden, Mrs. Sotheby with a basket and the general obediently clipping what she pointed out. And when Linda came out of Mrs. Bates's sitting room, where she had been getting final approval of her arrangements for the evening, they were still together. The general was praising one handsome vase that was intended for the sideboard while another, more magnificent bowl holding the dinner table centerpiece was taking shape under Mrs. Sotheby's fluttering but capable hands.

That problem was solved. Wondering if there were anything left to be done, Linda started and almost tripped over an uneven step when her name was called sharply. She turned to see Rose-Anne behind her at the top of the stairs.

"I want to talk to you," Rose-Anne said.

"Sure," Linda replied with assumed willingness. "Come down to the beach."

"No, I don't want my shoes full of sand, and I want to talk to you privately."

Linda was about to reply caustically but thought better of it. "All right," she said. "How about the gazebo?"

"Aunt Emmeline is too likely to interrupt us there. We can walk up the cliff. No one goes there except me."

Linda came back up the stairs slowly, annoyed, thinking that a bathing suit and towel were not very suitable clothing for hiking up a cliff. She could have used that excuse for refusing to go, but was reluctant to say no, though she knew that was foolish. If Rose-Anne was so set on privacy, she doubtless had something unpleasant to say. *Why should I give up my swim to listen to a scolding I don't deserve?* Linda asked herself resentfully. But she had a guilty feeling that she did deserve it for not warning

Donald away. Besides, she thought, maybe this will solve the problem. I can tell Rose-Anne I'm not interested, just friendly; maybe she'll pass the message along even if she doesn't completely believe me.

"Who were you looking for?" Rose-Anne asked as they walked past the gazebo.

"I wasn't looking *for* anyone," Linda hedged, as they went through the garden gate and began to climb a rather steep path.

"Come off it," Rose-Anne snapped. "I was watching you."

"That's nice," Linda replied sarcastically.

Either she had managed to put Rose-Anne at a disadvantage—or the precipitous path had silenced her. Linda's own breath was coming rather short when Rose-Anne stopped suddenly. Linda took another step and then stopped too. Rose-Anne's eyes were angry, and her mouth was set in a hard, unhappy line. Uncomfortably, Linda glanced down the path and saw with a shock that it had taken so sharp a turn that the house, the garden, and the lower part of the path itself were completely hidden from view. Slightly alarmed by the growing fury on Rose-Anne's face—the woman was certainly larger and stronger than she was—Linda took a hasty step backward.

"Be careful!" Rose-Anne cried, catching at her.

Linda gasped when she realized that the path was still turning and her backward step had carried her dangerously close to the edge. "This is no place to talk," she said breathlessly. But Rose-Anne was standing in the middle of the path, staring sightlessly right through her.

Was she regretting that she had pulled rather than pushed? Linda wondered, suddenly frightened and absolutely determined to escape from her precarious position. She would not pass Rose-Anne on the cliff side, so she used her towel as a shield and pushed her way past a low bush, intending to scramble up the bank and around the other side. To her surprise, what she had thought was a solid part of the hill turned out to be a massive boulder with another path on the other side that ran into the track they had climbed where it widened below. Because the hidden path was somewhat higher, Linda could now see the house and the entire track winding up the hill, and when Rose-Anne called, "Wait," Linda stopped, feeling a little foolish over her fear.

"I'm sorry," Rose-Anne said tightly. "I've got off on the wrong foot with you. I didn't mean to frighten you or offend you. If you want to know, I wasn't spying on you. I was watching for you so we could have this talk."

She paused and her face was so desperately unhappy that Linda would have helped her if she had known how.

"Oh, Donald is a louse!" Rose-Anne burst out. "And you don't understand about twins. I—I always help him, and he always helps me— even when we know the other is wrong. But— I can't. It's not fair!"

A Delicate Balance

Linda was so surprised at this turn in the conversation that she could do nothing except blink.

"Donald is in love with someone else. He's just using you," Rose-Anne went on desperately.

"Oh!" Linda exclaimed, and in the next moment grinned broadly. "Oh, that's wonderful!" She burst out laughing at Rose-Anne's stunned expression and put out her hand to the taller women. "I'm so glad you decided to tell me. You've saved me from really putting my foot in my mouth. You see, so am I—in love with someone else, I mean, and I haven't been able to find a tactful way to tell *Donald* not to get too involved with me. That's why I was sneaking out of the house. I wanted to stay out of your brother's way."

Rose-Anne breathed a long sigh of relief and leaned back against the boulder. "I think that's the hardest thing I've ever done. I never told a secret of Donald's before in my life. We've been arguing about this virtually since he met you." She scowled suddenly. "He knows too much about women. He kept saying that you'd be immune to his charm. I hate to admit he was right."

"Oh, you don't have to," Linda said, smiling. "You were right. I'd have succumbed if there hadn't already been someone else, and it wasn't kind of Donald to act as if he was interested. You were perfectly right to give him hell."

"It wasn't just for fun." Rose-Anne rushed to her twin's defense. "You see, my mother has this thing about actresses and Donald . . ." her voice faltered. "He . . . sometimes he does look for an easy way out. Instead of just telling Mother and waiting for the storm to subside—it would, as Mother can't bear to make either of us unhappy—he got this crazy idea that she would be so upset if he seemed to be courting you—because Mother is even worse on the subject of alliances with inferiors, like servants—that she would accept Diane gladly."

Linda began to laugh. "Poor Donald. I'll bet your mother never even noticed."

"No, she didn't," Rose-Anne agreed, raising her brows. "He thought she followed him that evening on the ship when I broke in on your drink so rudely. I'm sorry about that. I didn't know you were innoculated, and you're right about Donald's charm. But it wasn't my mother, if anyone was there. Mother was with me. Anyway, I told him Mother didn't regard you as a servant, and he was playing a dangerous game for nothing."

"It isn't because your mother doesn't regard me as a servant—" Linda began. Then she stopped, annoyed with herself. She didn't want to spoil Mrs. Sotheby's romance, and she wasn't sure how Rose-Anne would feel about that, even if she was a much nicer person than Linda had originally thought. But Linda needn't have been concerned. Rose-Anne's eyes brightened, and she cocked her head slightly in a gesture of amused interest.

"Oh, I say, do you think Mother and General Barthemeles are . . . er . . . making eyes at each other?"

Linda had to laugh at the deliberately antiquated slang, but she still was reluctant to say too much.

"It would be wonderful," Rose-Anne went on rather wistfully. "We worry about her, you know—I mean about her being lonely. Our lives are so different, and she doesn't understand or like our friends. We're being pulled apart all the time."

"Well," Linda said tentatively, "they were doing the flowers for the evening together when I left the house. He's lonely and wants someone to take care of—his attitude would drive me nuts, but your mother didn't seem to mind. Look, I'd better get back. I'll tell Donald I'm interested in someone else. Then if he still wants to use me as a lever, I don't mind, although I don't think it will do any good."

Rose-Anne smiled. "Maybe you'd better hint about Mother and the general—no, I'll tell him that, and it'll be more than a hint." Suddenly the smile was replaced with an expression of anxiety. "You won't tell him about this talk, will you?"

"No, of course not," Linda assured her. "I'll just say I felt we were seeing an awful lot of each other and I ought to warn him I was already spoken for."

"Thanks. You don't mind going back to the house yourself, do you? It isn't far. I have a friend who lives farther up on the hill. Since I've climbed this far, I might as well go all the way."

So that was where Rose-Anne had been so much of the time and why she was so familiar with this path, Linda thought, as she nodded. They waved a friendly goodbye to each other and parted. Linda was pleased and relieved. She wondered whether it was worthwhile to go back to her interrupted swim and then decided she'd better find Donald first. She was eager to clear up the situation so that she could explain it to Peter, but she needed Donald's agreement before she told Peter about his love affair.

Just as Linda came through the gate, she was aware of Donald heading for the beach. She didn't feel like shouting his name, so she ran after him. From the corner of her eye she saw someone coming off the verandah, but no one called and she continued along the path. She caught Donald just before he got into the water.

"Where have you been?" he asked. "I've been looking all over for you."

It was an excellent opening. Linda promptly admitted she had intended to avoid him and had then decided that it would be impossible, or at least awkward, when they were living in the same house.

"Avoid me? Why?"

"Because I've enjoyed your company and—and I wondered whether, perhaps, you enjoyed mine a little too much." Seeing the way Donald tensed, Linda said quickly, "You see, I can't—I'm in love with someone else."

"Oh," he said blankly.

For a second or two Linda wondered whether Rose-Anne knew her brother as well as she thought she did, but very soon Donald uttered a long sigh and a relieved and beatific smile covered his face. The sullenness that had seemed to underlie his expression, even when he was laughing, momentarily disappeared. Apparently, Donald's conscience had been pricking him more than Rose-Anne realized. In any case, the whole story tumbled out of him and his apology for "using" Linda was full and fervent.

"That's all right." She laughed, and then decided that in view of his own need for secrecy it was unlikely that Donald would spill the beans about her. "Look," she said, "we can go on playing this game if you like, but I have to tell Peter. He's getting jealous."

"I had noticed," Donald remarked drily. "In fact, I've been wondering whether he was going to murder me. That, among other things, has given me second thoughts about the whole idea. Rose-Anne didn't like it, and if she criticizes something I do, it has to be really off. But if you don't mind—and if you can get Peter to stop glaring at me—sure, tell him about Diane. He's a lucky man, Linda. You're quite a girl."

In an excess of good feeling, they kissed. Then Linda pulled away, looked at the sun, and gasped. "I've got to get back to the house. There's the table to check, and I've got to see if Mrs. Bates has any last-minute instructions for me."

She ran hastily up the steps, watching her footing because the uneven stone stairs were not designed for speed. At the top of the flight, Linda raised her head just in time to save herself from literally running into Peter. He was furious—white with rage, eyes blazing.

"Oh, Peter," Linda gasped, torn between her need to get back to the house and her duties there and her desire to explain what had happened. "It wasn't what you thought. Donald isn't interested in me at all."

"He has one hell of a funny way of showing it," Peter snarled.

"I haven't time to explain now. I've got to get back and make sure everything's ready for the dinner tonight. Look, as soon as the party's over, I'll meet you in the gazebo. It's a long story, and a kind of funny one. You'll enjoy it."

But Peter was in no mood to listen to funny stories or to wait to hear one. Seeing how angry he still was, Linda would have told him more—at least enough to pacify him—but she was facing the house and saw Mrs. Bates step off the verandah and glance around.

"There's your aunt, looking for me," she said, and moved to step around Peter.

The movement to escape him increased his fury so much that he was deaf to what she had said. He grasped her arm brutally tight and wrenched her back toward him so that

Linda uttered a sharp cry, expressing equally shock and pain.

"What kind of a sucker—" Peter had begun when Mrs. Bates's voice peremptorily calling Linda's name made him half turn his head and relax his grip.

Linda pulled her arm free. "I'll see you in the gazebo later," she hissed, then called aloud, "Here I am, Mrs. Bates. Sorry I forgot the time. I'm coming."

When Linda reached her, Mrs. Bates said stiffly, "Is Peter annoying you, Linda?"

"Oh, no!" Linda exclaimed, but she could feel herself blushing.

"I want you to know that there is no need to endure my nephew's importunities in order to retain your position with me," Mrs. Bates said forcefully. "In fact, it is my duty to protect you against him, and I shall do so."

"He didn't mean anything, Mrs. Bates," Linda soothed. "He was in the middle of a sentence and didn't want me to leave."

"So I see," Mrs. Bates remarked acidly, her eyes on Linda's bare arm where the marks of Peter's fingers still showed red. "I will make sure," she said austerely, "that such behavior does not happen again."

"It's nothing." Linda laughed easily. "Honestly. You know how clumsy he is. I'm sure he had no intention of hurting me. In another minute he would have been confounding himself in apologies. I like Peter. And I can take care of myself. Please don't give it another thought."

Mrs. Bates said no more about Peter, changing the subject to the final arrangements for dinner. Fortunately, as it was nearly time to dress, she was in general very pleased. The few suggestions she had for changes in Linda's plans took only moments to carry out and Linda was free to change her clothes. She grinned as she put away the sleeveless blouse she had planned to wear and took out a long-sleeved lace affair. Peter's fingermarks had already upset Mrs. Bates enough. They didn't need to become public. He really grabbed me, Linda thought, looking at the bruises, which were already changing from red to black-and-blue. She hoped he wouldn't disgrace himself further by acting silly at dinner.

If Peter didn't actually disgrace himself, he came close to it. His eyes were glaring, his lips thinned to an ugly line, and the best that could be won from him in conversation was a disgruntled monosyllable. Fortunately, everyone else was in very high spirits indeed. Donald and Rose-Anne were bubbling with laughter and smart remarks that were, for once, completely good-natured. Mrs. Paxton, her brother, and his son and daughter were very ready to join in the hilarity. And from the glow in Mrs. Sotheby's eyes and the gleam in the general's, Linda guessed that the flowers might have brought the gentleman to a declaration.

It was pleasant, Linda thought, to be able to relax. The party was going very well without any application of social oil. She was more annoyed than sorry that Peter was wrapped in his own little black cloud. All would be explained soon enough, and he was too old to inflict private woes on guests. What troubled Linda more than Peter's sulks was that Mrs. Bates was not acting as sprightly as usual. Not that she seemed ill; her color was good and she was alert, not dazed. At first Linda had felt a bit guilty, thinking Mrs. Bates was worried about her, but she soon intercepted a couple of glances that indicated it was the open understanding between Mrs. Sotheby and the general that had disturbed her.

Linda was saddened. There did not seem to be any jealousy or anger in Mrs. Bates's occasional glances. What showed on her face in the few unguarded moments when her social mask dropped was loneliness and fear. Her sister-in-law and her friend had drawn together. She, who had been the center around which their relationship had developed, was now outside. Linda felt Mrs. Bates was mistaken. She believed that Mrs. Sotheby and the general would be better company for her now that their own problems were out of the way.

It was unfortunate, Linda thought, that there was no way for her to assure Mrs. Bates of that. And it was really infuriating that Peter, usually so alert to his aunt's needs, had chosen this evening to yield to the green-eyed devil. Now, if ever, Mrs. Bates needed a warm glance and a laughing word of affection—and she was getting nothing. Linda had noticed that each time Mrs. Bates's eyes slid away from Mrs. Sotheby's happy smile, they glanced at Peter. Linda got angrier and angrier each time he failed to respond; either he didn't raise his head from his food or his eyes stared unseeingly right past his aunt.

Chapter Seventeen

All in all, Linda was rather glad when the Paxton ménage left, even though they were pleasant people and the party had gone well. Rose-Anne and Donald decided to accompany Mrs. Paxton's nephew and niece into town to finish the evening at a night spot there. Linda refused their invitation with a polite excuse, and Peter just growled, "No," and stomped off into the small study that adjoined the dining room, which was sometimes used for writing letters.

Mrs. Bates had at first urged Linda to go with the other young people and frowned when she refused. But then she sighed and conceded that Linda must be tired after working so hard all day. She thanked her for the care and attention that had made the dinner progress so smoothly.

Linda made a laughing remark about that being what she was paid for and barely stopped herself from approving with far too much enthusiasm when Mrs. Bates nodded and said, "I think I will go to bed now."

In the next moment, Linda was thoroughly ashamed when she saw Mrs. Bates's eyes wander to the general and Mrs. Sotheby, who were sitting on the sofa talking eagerly. Peter, who had been thoroughly inconsiderate of his aunt, could wait a few minutes more, she thought, and asked gently, "Would you like me to read to you for a while?"

"No, my dear, I'm tired. You are a good girl, Linda. I wish you were my daughter."

Linda clamped her teeth over the words that she might be as good as a daughter soon. She thought Mrs. Bates did look tired, and should not be exposed to any more emotional strain. But she really couldn't think of any other answer to such a remark, so she just squeezed her employer's hand gently. She had looked down and almost missed the quick glance Mrs. Bates cast at the door through which Peter had gone. Then the old lady's eyes returned to her, and she stared at Linda rather oddly.

"You have no parents," she murmured, her voice so low Linda had to strain to hear her. Clearly she was talking as much to herself as to Linda. "And I have no child." Her eyes flicked to the door to the writing room again. "Something—something might be worked out . . . something . . . safe."

When Mrs. Bates had first looked after Peter and then stared at her, Linda had felt a warm rush of pleasure. It seemed for that instant that news of the relationship between her and Peter would be more welcome than she had expected. But the old lady's last words about "something . . . safe" had sent a sudden chill through her. Her lips parted to speak, but she found she had nothing to say; she swallowed hard and cleared her throat lightly.

As if the soft sound had brought her to herself, Mrs. Bates laughed somewhat self-consciously and murmured, "I really am tired. Good night, my dear."

Linda went slowly up to her room to get a jacket. The days were warm, almost hot, but the nights were cool. Her hand fell on her navy blue raincoat, and she slipped it on. It was not very appropriate with a long black skirt but her working-girl front did not run to an evening cloak, and the wooly white coat she had worn in England's autumn weather was too warm. Besides, it would stand out like a beacon in the moonlight.

She made her way down the stairs cautiously. It would be easy enough to say she was going out for a walk if anyone asked, but Linda preferred not to tell lies, even innocent ones, if she could avoid them. The dining room was dark, the servants finished clearing, she was glad to see, and she moved through it carefully, closing the glass doors gently behind her. When she was about halfway down to the gazebo,

Linda thought she heard the latch click and she glanced back quickly, wondering if she had not shut the door properly. The moon was bright in the garden, but it was too dark on the verandah to see whether the door had sprung open. Linda hesitated, then decided it didn't matter. She was certain the door would not slide all the way open, and it wasn't likely that a thief would try the house when so many lights were still burning.

A minute later, Linda was at the gazebo. Her first reaction was a twinge of disappointment because she thought the place was empty, but then a crouching shadow moved on the far side of the screened structure. Linda stopped short, her heart suddenly pounding. Why should anyone crouch in the shadows? Her immediate impulse was to run back to the house, but then she began to move softly around to where she would be able to see through the screen. Whoever it was would have to open the door on the other side and come around the gazebo to get at her, and she was sure she would have time to scream and run before she could be caught. Her curiosity was greater than her fear.

She rounded the side of the gazebo, walking softly, but the figure's head was bent and the little moonlight that got through the screens made it impossible to see hair color. What she did see was the gleam of metal in one hand. Linda's breath caught. A knife? She stepped back incautiously and a twig snapped. The head flung up, and Peter's face was white in the moonlight.

He stood up abruptly. "What the hell are you doing on this side?" he asked sharply, but in a very low voice. "Do you want to fall off that damned cliff? Go around and come in here."

"What are you doing?" Linda asked, little above a whisper.

"Fixing this damned lock. The screws have been taken out and the holes filled with dirt. I saw it when I came out to meet you and I went back and got the stuff to fix it from Yani. Come in here. I've got a flashlight, but I can't hold it and the screw and screwdriver all at the same time."

Linda stood perfectly still, her eyes staring with horror. "No," she whispered. "No! If your aunt had leaned on that door—and I've seen her do it—she would have fallen out. No! This has gone too far. Who did it?"

"Don't be an idiot, Linda. Come in here."

"No. How do I know *you* didn't take out those screws right now?"

"Oh, you damn fool!" Peter's voice grated. He pushed the screwdriver into his pocket and came toward her. His hand was extended, and on the palm were three bright new screws. Obviously those had never come out of an old rusted lock.

Nonetheless, Linda backed away. She was not afraid of Peter; she was furious with him. "No," she repeated. "I won't be a party to this any more. It's too dangerous. If you won't tell me who's doing this, I'm going to go to the police. I don't care whether they think I'm crazy or not. Then I'm going to tell your aunt that I'm quitting. I won't sit around and wait till a murder happens. If I can't stop it, at least I won't condone it."

She turned and began to run toward the house. Behind her she heard Peter call, "Linda!" in a furious voice, and then heard the door of the gazebo slam. As angry as Linda was, she had no intention of exposing Mrs. Bates to a violent scene between her and Peter, and she was afraid he was now enraged enough not to care about anything. She veered from the direct path to the verandah and made for the garden gate. As she opened it, the sitting room door opened, the stream of light showing the general shepherding Mrs. Sotheby out onto the west verandah. A vagrant breeze pulled the door from the general's hand and it slammed.

Linda slipped through the gate and closed it silently behind her. She started up the steep path, walking carefully so that she would make no noise, aware that her black skirt and dark raincoat would make her almost invisible if she kept to the shadows. She felt an urgent need to be alone. Something in Peter's exasperated tone as he called her a damn fool had increased her anger because it started a completely new and very unpleasant train of thought.

She heard Peter call her name again, but she did not reply, taking the inner path, away from the cliff edge, until she came to the rock she had discovered when she was with Rose-Anne that morning. She stepped behind it. She didn't want

Peter to find her. She needed to think—hard.

For a few seconds, Linda hoped Peter had gone back into the house, but then the moonlight caught his white shirt as he came through the gate and started up the path at a loping stride. "God damn it, Linda," he called, "come back. This path is dangerous at night."

He was just below her now on the outer path. Linda bit her lip. That path was dangerous, and Peter was so clumsy. She took a breath to answer him but was startled into silence by Mrs. Bates's voice.

"She isn't up there. I heard her go into the house."

From Linda's vantage point, she could see the old woman come out of the gate and start upward on the path. Linda shrank back, around the boulder; she couldn't see from there, but she was certain she couldn't be seen either. The last thing she wanted was to be caught in concealment, as if she had been intending to eavesdrop.

"For God's sake, Aunt Em," Linda heard Peter exclaim. "Don't come up here. Don't climb the hill. I'll come down."

"No, no." The sweet voice, nearer now and not at all breathless, was reproving. "You stay right where you are."

Linda thought she heard Peter make a muffled exclamation, but Mrs. Bates's voice almost covered the sound. "I have to kill you, Peter," the old woman said with a loud sigh. "I'm sorry, you know, truly sorry, but I need the money.

Everyone is leaving me. I need the money to pay Gertrude and Linda and the people I will need to take care of me when I become helpless. You see, there isn't anything wrong with my heart. I know that. I'll live a long time, and there won't be enough."

Linda's mouth dropped open and she turned to stare but all she saw was the boulder and the brush that surrounded it. She was so shocked that she didn't realize she hadn't moved.

"There'll be enough, Aunt Em." Peter's voice was shaking. "I swear there will be. I'll—"

"No. You are lying again. I don't like it when you lie to me, Peter. George and Peter should never have made that agreement. The business should have come to me, not been willed to you. George had no right to leave Bates Limited to his sister's son. Why, you could cut me off without a shilling any time you please."

"It isn't true, Aunt Em. Your income is settled on you. I can't touch that. Uncle George wouldn't leave you unprotected. Your own solicitor explained it to you."

Linda stood silent, grateful now that she had not moved and was still hidden from them both. The poor woman was deranged! Whatever Mrs. Bates had had, stroke or attack, it had damaged her mind. Then Peter must have moved, because Mrs. Bates cried out angrily.

"Don't you come down," she ordered. "You have to stay there because it would be too much for me to push you off the cliff from down here. It was convenient that you mistreated Linda today. It will be a good reason. I had to stop you from pursuing her. And everyone knows you've been trying to kill me for months. I had to protect both of us, didn't I?"

"Don't climb the hill," Peter said. "Let me come down, and I'll go into the gazebo with you."

Linda pressed a hand to her mouth to hold back sobs. Mrs. Bates was the one who had removed the screws. Had she intended to push Peter out the door? But even as she thought it, she realized something was wrong. If Peter didn't want his aunt to climb the hill, why didn't he just go down? Linda stepped forward, and a tough branch tangled in her coat. She heard running steps and pulled fiercely at the coat as she heard Peter cry out, "Don't, please don't."

With a mighty wrench, Linda struggled free and came around the rock above him, only to freeze with horror. Her mouth opened, but no sound would come from her paralyzed throat. Mrs. Bates was now running, nearly leaping, up the final yards of the slope that separated her from Peter—and she had a short, gleaming pistol in her hand.

"Don't run, Aunt Em, don't run!" Peter shouted, holding his hands palm out as if to push his aunt back.

The pistol cracked. Linda, unable to scream, managed to run forward, but she was too far away to push Peter down, out of the way of the bullet. Peter was still standing, still gesturing, still crying out—insanely—"Don't run!

Don't run!" And Mrs. Bates fired again, and again, almost point blank. Peter staggered back.

Freed at last, Linda screamed, but Peter did not fall. He caught himself upright, one hand against the boulder. It was Mrs. Bates whose stride checked suddenly. In the next second, she went rigid, then collapsed before Peter, who had thrust himself toward her, could catch her. He seemed to fall forward then, almost on top of his aunt, and Linda flew over the distance between them, dropping to her knees beside him.

"Oh, my God," Peter groaned, his voice ragged with sobs.

"Where are you hurt?" Linda cried, grabbing at him.

There were tears running down his cheeks. "If I'd stayed in the gazebo," he whispered. "She wouldn't have run up the hill."

"Peter, where are you hurt?" Linda screamed, shaking him. "I saw her fire at you point-blank."

Slowly he reached forward and took the gun out of his aunt's hand. He held the wrist, then laid her hand gently down and wiped his face. "I'm sorry, Linda," he said softly. "I'm sorry we frightened you. I'm not hurt at all. Maybe a bruise from that last shot that was so close. I had put blanks in the gun a long time ago. I kept telling you I was in no danger."

The garden gate opened noisily, and the general came charging through. "Peter!" he bellowed. "Where are you? Are you all right?"

"I'm all right," Peter called huskily, and then, choking, "Aunt Em's dead."

A Delicate Balance

The general paused half-way up, turned around, and bellowed down the hill, "Harriet, tell one of the maids to send a man for the police and a doctor." Then he came up the rest of the way and glared around. "Heard the gun go off." He spotted it in Peter's hand. "Damn fool," he growled, "give that thing to me to clean. Hurry up. You want the police to see you carrying it?"

"You knew too?" Linda gasped.

"Poor child," the general said more gently, "what a shock you've had. Take her back to the house and get her a drink, Peter. Here, give me that gun." He took it from Peter's nerveless fingers. "You'd better have a drink yourself."

"I should have stayed in the gazebo," Peter repeated dully.

"Now don't you be a fool, young man," the General boomed. "She was gettin' worse and worse. If she had hurt you, she would have had to be locked up. This is better. I was gettin' damned worried, I can tell you."

"I would never have locked her up," Peter said, "no matter what. For years she was so wonderful. When I first came to England, you don't know how wonderful she was. So she had a stroke six months ago—so she got a little queer. I couldn't have locked her up like a mad dog."

"Know Emmeline a good deal longer than you do," General Barthemeles said harshly. "Know what she did for me when m'wife was dyin' by inches. My memory's no shorter than yours, so I was willin' to keep my mouth shut and watch her while she tried to make everyone believe you were tryin' to kill her—to give her an excuse to kill you, I guess. But she was gettin' worse, Peter, not better. Stop rippin' yourself up for what had to happen. Take the gel back to the house."

At last Peter pulled his eyes from his aunt's still face. Linda put her arm around his waist, and he responded by pulling her to him so fiercely that she thought her ribs would crack. Then he sighed and released her, and they started to walk down the path.

The shock Linda had suffered had been violent, but as it receded, it seemed to have cleared her mind. So many unreasonable little things became quite—well, not reasonable, but explicable—in terms of Mrs. Bates casting suspicion on Peter. That stumble on the stairs that had started Linda wondering: when she saw Linda on the stairs in a position to catch her, Mrs. Bates had just let herself slip. Maybe it was Peter's shadow Linda had seen, but he had to have been in the drawing room with the light behind him, not out on the landing. And the candy that had made Gert so sleepy—

Peter was breathing oddly. Linda thought he might be crying. It would be a good thing if she could distract his mind from his "guilt" in letting his aunt run up the hill, but she knew she could never get him to think about anything but Mrs. Bates right now.

"Peter, where did your aunt get the drug she put in the candy and gave Gertrude on the ship?" Linda asked.

A Delicate Balance

"My uncle died of cancer," Peter replied wearily. "Aunt Em kept the stuff. At first it was because she couldn't part with anything of his. Then I think she forgot it was there. I guess I should have cleaned out the cabinet while she was in hospital after she had that stroke, but I never thought . . ." He sighed, shivered, and pulled Linda a little closer. "There wasn't any trouble about money, you know. It's true I own the business, but her income was fixed by my uncle's will—and even if she spent more, it wouldn't have mattered. I would have paid the bills. She didn't have to ask me for anything."

He sighed again, but his voice was already better, still husky but no longer hushed as if he could hardly bear to speak at all. Linda pursued the topic. "She pushed you on the ship, didn't she? Why, in heaven's name? Surely she must have known you couldn't go over the rail."

"I don't think she did know." Peter's lips twitched, almost finding a reminiscent smile. "She wasn't great at engineering. I was leaning pretty far over and I don't think she understood things like center of gravity." He shivered again. "And, well, I don't think she was thinking about anything very clearly."

"The thing that really bothered me was the way she was lying so nice and flat that last afternoon on the ship," Linda said next. "Even if someone had deliberately frightened her— which was what I thought at the time—I couldn't understand why the person would have stopped to straighten her out. I guess she just lay down

273

comfortably, but who called Gertrude and told her you wanted to see her?"

"A steward. I checked, just to make sure that there wasn't any funny business going on that I didn't know about. She gave the fellow a pound to make the call. She didn't even think of trying to hide the trail. Poor Aunt Em."

That sounded much better to Linda. There was grief in his voice, but the agonized guilt that had choked him on the hill was gone. Linda looked at him tenderly as they came in the sitting room door. As horrible as the evening had been, it certainly portended a happy future for her. Peter really loved with all his heart and soul when he loved. Linda could not help smiling a little. Imagine feeling guilty because you hadn't let your aunt shoot you on a level spot.

She made him a drink and had one herself. Then they sat silently holding hands on a sofa until they heard a car on the gravel driveway. Peter started to get up, but Linda held him when she heard the clack of a woman's heels going to the door. After a few minutes, Mrs. Sotheby came in.

"That was the police with a doctor. They are going directly up the hill and will want to talk to us when they come back."

Peter said nothing but got to his feet and stared out the dark window.

"I've told Gertrude," Mrs. Sotheby continued in a lower voice to Linda, "but I don't know whether she took it in. I think Emmeline must have given her something to make her sleep again. I liked Emmeline, you know. She was a really good person. She tried to help me when my own brother wouldn't even say my name, and she finally made him forgive me—though I'll never know what I did to injure him. But after that stroke . . . She frightened me."

"I don't think she was dangerous to anyone but Peter," Linda said. "Maybe it was because she loved him so much that he became the focus of her paranoia when her mind was damaged."

"Perhaps." But Mrs. Sotheby sounded doubtful. "Only she seemed to have lost . . . I don't know . . . a sense of balance. She could only see what she wanted whether or not it was reasonable or dangerous to someone else. This business of drugging Gertrude all the time. What if she had used too much? I think Gertrude knew, too. I don't think she will take Emmeline's death as hard as she would have some time ago. She has been frightened for some time—since her niece got that drugged candy. She was too loyal to desert Emmeline, but—Oh, I hear Cecil's voice. Will you stay with Peter? Are you all right?"

Linda nodded and Mrs. Sotheby hurried out. Linda went to the window and took Peter's hand in hers. He put his head down on the top of hers for a moment, then led her back to the sofa. Again they waited for what seemed like a long time.

"What do you think—" Peter had just begun to say when he was interrupted by the entrance of two men, one in uniform and one in plain clothes.

The plainclothesman introduced himself in fluent, if accented English and then asked, "You were with Mrs. Bates when she died?"

"Yes," Peter and Linda responded together.

"Ah, yes. The doctor tells me she died of a brain seizure, that she had one before, and that at her age another was to be expected."

So the Corfu doctor was not such a fool, Linda thought.

"Yes, she had a very bad stroke previously," Peter agreed.

"Ah, so you knew that, yes? Our doctor says there was nothing he could do except advise her against exertion. What was she doing on that hill?"

Peter closed his eyes and swallowed. "It was my fault," he said miserably.

"No," Linda interrupted. "It was my fault."

Peter was going to say something stupid, and this poor policeman, who simply wanted something to put into his report would hear the whole ugly-sad story. No one was guilty of anything, not even poor Mrs. Bates, who had only been sick, and there was no reason to generate a scandal in this tight little colony where she and Peter and Rose-Anne and the others might want to come again.

"Mr. Tattersall and I are going to be married," Linda continued before Peter could get a word in, "but we hadn't yet told Mrs. Bates. This afternoon, Mr. Tattersall and I had a silly argument, and he gripped my arm." Linda lifted her sleeve to show her bruises. She heard Peter's breath hiss in with great satisfaction. That would give him something fresh—and much healthier—to be guilty about.

"Mrs. Bates saw this. She asked me whether Mr. Tattersall was annoying me. Although I assured her he was not and it had been an accident, I was so angry with him that I did not tell her we were betrothed. At dinner tonight, Mr. Tattersall behaved like a boor and made me even angrier. When I went out later for a walk, he followed me. We had another few words—rather sharp ones—and I left to walk along the cliff. Mr. Tattersall felt that it was too dangerous to walk there at night and he went after me. Mrs. Bates must have believed that he was pursuing me and she followed. By the time we noticed her—" Linda stopped and waited for her voice to steady, suppressing the remembered horror of the true event. "It was too late."

"Ah, I see. The poor lady. At least she did not suffer at all." He nodded and made a few notes on a small pad that Linda had not previously noticed. "So, a natural death by—ah, yes—the English word, I believe is, misadventure. At the—you would call it the Town Hall—if you wish to bury her here or take her home, there you must make the arrangements."

"Yes," Peter said.

The policeman bowed. "My sympathy," he said, and withdrew.

Peter started to move toward the window to stare out again, but Linda caught at his arm. "It was nobody's fault," she said sharply. "Why didn't you tell me she had had a stroke right away instead of saying she had had a heart attack? I couldn't see any symptoms of a weak heart, and I wondered why you had lied."

"I knew that," Peter said "but I thought it was more important that you shouldn't think she was a mental case or be afraid of her. In fact, I'd decided I had to tell you tonight. I was thinking about it all through dinner, and when you asked whether I had taken the screws out of the lock, I knew I had to tell you. Up till then, I was sure you weren't in any danger and, if you remember, in the beginning I did try to get rid of you. But she had attached herself so strongly to you—Aunt Em always had good taste." He started to laugh and the sound caught into a sob.

"She attached herself to me as a substitute for you."

"That could be," he agreed, and then burst out bitterly, "Oh, God, I wish I hadn't gone up that hill."

"For heaven's sake, Peter," Linda said impatiently, "if you want the ugly truth, I probably killed her by screaming. She didn't know I was there, and that shock, added to the climb, almost certainly raised her blood pressure enough to burst another vessel in her brain. Do you want me to go and confess to murder?"

"You mustn't feel like that, Linda," Peter murmured anxiously, putting his arms around her.

"It wasn't you, and it had to happen pretty soon anyway."

Linda made no reply to his comforting remarks. She felt no guilt at all and had only said what she did to force Peter to recognize his own innocence and the inevitability of his aunt's death. It took him a moment longer to hear his own words, then he smiled wryly.

"I'm a fool," he said. "It's just that I'll miss her so. She *is* better off. She wasn't happy, Linda. She really was sorry about trying to kill me."

"Yes," Linda agreed at once. "The sane part of her loved you." And then Linda realized that the police might check on her because she had given evidence, and she was reminded that she had a secret she had better tell him. It was a good time, too. It would give him something to think about beside his aunt's death, yet he wouldn't be able to think about it enough to get angry. "Peter," she said urgently, then stopped.

He looked surprised at the urgency of her tone and at the sudden hesitation, releasing her so that he could look down into her face. "Yes?"

"There's something I'd better tell you that you don't know about me. If the police start to investigate—although I don't know why they should—they'll find out, and I don't want you to get another shock."

"You've been married before?"

"Oh, no!" Linda exclaimed. "I would have told you anything *personal*. This is nothing to do with me, really, only that I'm—well, I've got money."

"Money?" Peter echoed blankly.

"Maybe you'll think I'm rich—or maybe only just wealthy. I'm worth a few million."

"Million?" Peter repeated, then exploded, "What the hell were you doing working for my aunt and borrowing money for an evening skirt?"

Linda knew she looked sheepish; she felt silly. "I—I just wanted a job. I wanted to do something really demeaning to make me appreciate what I had." A gobbling sound of pure incredulity came from Peter and she hurried on, trying to make what she had done sound reasonable. "I thought I needed a worm's eye view of life and I thought the lowest worm you could be was a companion, so . . . well, who would hire me as a companion if she knew I had money or turned up in a Dior dress?"

Peter found his voice. "You're nuts!"

"I am not!" Linda said indignantly. "You have money too—or at least I guess you have a good business from the style in which your aunt lived—but you always worked for it. I was just born with it. I—"

"Do your parents—the ones you told Aunt Em were dead—know about this?"

Linda drew herself up righteously. "I do not tell lies. My parents *are* dead. They died when I was about a year old." Then she grinned at Peter. "Of course, my Aunt Evelyn and Uncle Abe, who brought me up, would agree with you. But I didn't tell them. I wasn't doing anything criminal, you know. I just wanted to find out what I was good for—and I found out. I'm a born organizer and administrator. I think I might go into garbage disposal or . . ."

Peter was staring at her with a kind of glaze over his eyes, and Linda poked him gently in the ribs.

"Or maybe TV," she said provocatively. "I wonder how I'd do on the production side. I guess I'd have a crack in the door to sneak in, since I have a relative involved."

"Donald!" Peter snarled, snapping back to life. "I forgot about him. What the hell were you two up to on the beach?"

"We were congratulating each other," Linda said blandly. "Donald told me he wants to marry a girl called Diane, and I told him I wanted to marry you."

"He was using you," Peter said angrily.

Linda laughed. "No more than I was using him. Even-Steven, Peter."

He still looked angry when he opened his mouth, but what came out was not another furious tirade, but a hearty laugh. Then, shocked by the sound, he sobered. "You certainly are a born administrator," he remarked. "You've administered a good dose of sense to me. It's all right, darling. You don't have to make any more horrid confessions. Aunt Em's dead, and I've accepted it."

"She isn't dead, Peter," Linda said softly, "only the bad part. All the good of her is alive in your memory and the general's and Mrs. Sotheby's— even in mine. I knew her just enough to want to know more."

Peter nodded and drew her close again. "As soon as I've made the arrangements and we've done what we must, we'll fly to the States so your aunt and uncle can meet me. I want to be married as soon as I can get them to agree."

Linda smiled tenderly at him. "That won't take long. Aunt Evelyn's so eager to see me in white that she may not let you leave the house until the knot is tied."

AMII LORIN

Don't miss these novels of undying love by the bestselling author of more than 5 million books in print!

"Amii Lorin always gives her readers something special!"
—Romantic Times

While The Fire Rages. Charming and attentive one minute, angry and suspicious the next, Brett Renninger is impossible to work for—and even more impossible to resist. Despite the intoxicating madness Brett's passionate kisses rouse in her, young executive Jo Lawrence fears that he has hidden secrets that will destroy their chance at everlasting love.
_3369-0 $3.99 US/$4.99 CAN

Come Home To Love. Katherine Acker is stunned when ruthless entrepreneur Matthew Martin offers to marry her if she will act as a hostess to his business associates. Little does Katherine know that Matt has more surprises in store for her—and one of them may be that he loves her....
_3317-8 $3.99 US/$4.99 CAN

PLAYING FOR KEEPS/
A TEMPTING STRANGER
Lori Copeland

Two Complete Romances—
A $7.98 Value For Only $4.50!

PLAYING FOR KEEPS

When she was just seventeen, Jessica Cole married the only man she had ever loved, but fate intervened and they were divorced almost immediately. Now, eight years later, Jason Rawlings is back. He thinks he can toy with her, but Jessica is tired of heartbreak—this time she is playing for keeps.

A TEMPTING STRANGER

Her wedding only weeks away, Chandra Long agrees to pose as a stranger's wife. But when she takes to her part too well, Garrett Morganson won't let her go. Chandra knows she should accept the security her fiance offers, but how can she forget the seductive stranger who has stolen her heart?

__3380-1 $4.50

SPEND YOUR LEISURE MOMENTS WITH US.

Hundreds of exciting titles to choose from—something for everyone's taste in fine books: breathtaking historical romance, chilling horror, spine-tingling suspense, taut medical thrillers, involving mysteries, action-packed men's adventure and wild Westerns.

SEND FOR A FREE CATALOGUE TODAY!

Leisure Books
Attn: Customer Service Department
276 5th Avenue, New York, NY 10001